I0633555

Old School Tales

Ruskin Bond is known for his signature simplistic and witty writing style. He is the author of several bestselling short stories, novellas, collections, essays and children's books and has contributed a number of poems and articles to various magazines and anthologies. At the age of twenty-three, he won the prestigious John Llewellyn Rhys Prize for his first novel, *The Room on the Roof*. He was also the recipient of the Padma Shri in 1999, Lifetime Achievement Award by the Delhi Government in 2012 and the Padma Bhushan in 2014.

Born in 1934, Ruskin Bond grew up in Jamnagar, Shimla, New Delhi and Dehradun. Apart from three years in the UK, he has spent all his life in India, and now lives in Landour, Mussoorie, with his adopted family.

RUSKIN BOND

Old School Tales

RUPA

Published by
Rupa Publications India Pvt. Ltd 2023
7/16, Ansari Road, Daryaganj
New Delhi 110002

Sales centres:
Prayagraj Bengaluru Chennai
Hyderabad Jaipur Kathmandu
Kolkata Mumbai

This is a work of fiction. Names, characters, places and incidents are either the product of the author's imagination or are used fictitiously and any resemblance to any actual person, living or dead, events or locales is entirely coincidental.

P-ISBN: 978-93-5702-186-9
E-ISBN: 978-93-5702-183-8

First impression 2023

10 9 8 7 6 5 4 3 2 1

CONTENTS

INTRODUCTION

Remember waking up in the wee hours of the morning to rush to school after a hurried breakfast and then sauntering back home with friends on hot afternoons with ice creams dripping down our fingers? Schools bring a mixed bag of emotions and experiences for everyone—they can be full of fun and frolic while plaguing us with worries about examinations and strict teachers. However, once we pass out, we tend to look back on our school days with great nostalgia and fondness, reminiscing about the carefree days of mischief and laughter, unaffected by the worries of adulthood.

During my own time at boarding school in Shimla, I found the best of friends with whom I went on many wild escapades that not only brought me immense joy but also taught me a lot. I came across eccentric teachers, whose wisdom still remains with me. Above all, I forged an inseparable bond with nature at school, surrounded by the magnificent trees and wildlife of the Himalayas.

In *Old School Tales*, I have curated a collection of my writing reminiscing about school days. Some of the stories in this book—like 'From the Pool to the Glacier', 'Be Prepared' and 'The Four Feathers'—narrate bold exploits at or after school. Other stories—like 'The Long Day' and 'Our Great Escape'—explore the challenges of school life, from failing examinations to losing close friends.

I hope these tales take you back to days of wonder and

abandon, reminding you of simpler times when your biggest worry would be your mathematics homework and a romp with your friends on the school playground would make your day.

Ruskin Bond

THE SCHOOL AMONG THE PINES

1

A leopard, lithe and sinewy, drank at the mountain stream, and then lay down on the grass to bask in the late February sunshine. Its tail twitched occasionally and the animal appeared to be sleeping. At the sound of distant voices it raised its head to listen, then stood up and leapt lightly over the boulders in the stream, disappearing among the trees on the opposite bank.

A minute or two later, three children came walking down the forest path. They were a girl and two boys, and they were singing in their local dialect an old song they had learnt from their grandparents.

Five more miles to go!
We climb through rain and snow.
A river to cross…
A mountain to pass…
Now we've four more miles to go!

Their school satchels looked new, their clothes had been washed and pressed. Their loud and cheerful singing startled a Spotted Forktail. The bird left its favourite rock in the stream and flew down the dark ravine.

'Well, we have only three more miles to go,' said the bigger boy, Prakash, who had been this way hundreds of times. 'But first we have to cross the stream.'

He was a sturdy twelve-year-old with eyes like raspberries and a mop of bushy hair that refused to settle down on his head. The girl and her small brother were taking this path for the first time.

'I'm feeling tired, Bina,' said the little boy.

Bina smiled at him, and Prakash said, 'Don't worry, Sonu, you'll get used to the walk. There's plenty of time.' He glanced at the old watch he'd been given by his grandfather. It needed constant winding. 'We can rest here for five or six minutes.'

They sat down on a smooth boulder and watched the clear water of the shallow stream tumbling downhill. Bina examined the old watch on Prakash's wrist. The glass was badly scratched and she could barely make out the figures on the dial. 'Are you sure it still tells the right time?' she asked.

'Well, it loses five minutes every day, so I put it ten minutes forward at night. That means by morning it's quite accurate! Even our teacher, Mr Mani, asks me for the time. If he doesn't ask, I tell him! The clock in our classroom keeps stopping.'

They removed their shoes and let the cold mountain water run over their feet. Bina was the same age as Prakash. She had pink cheeks, soft brown eyes and hair that was just beginning to lose its natural curls. Hers was a gentle face, but a determined little chin showed that she could be a strong person. Sonu, her younger brother, was ten. He was a thin boy who had been sickly as a child but was now beginning to fill out. Although he did not look very athletic, he could run like the wind.

Bina had been going to school in her own village of Koli, on the other side of the mountain. But it had been a primary school, finishing at class five. Now, in order to study in the sixth grade, she would have to walk several miles every day to

Nauti, where there was a high school going up to the eighth grade. It had been decided that Sonu would also shift to the new school, to give Bina company. Prakash, their neighbour in Koli, was already a pupil at the Nauti school. His mischievous nature, which sometimes got him into trouble, had resulted in his having to repeat a year.

But this didn't seem to bother him. 'What's the hurry?' he had told his indignant parents. 'You're not sending me to a foreign land when I finish school. And our cows aren't running away, are they?'

'You would prefer to look after the cows, wouldn't you?' asked Bina, as they got up to continue their walk.

'Oh, school's all right. Wait till you see old Mr Mani. He always gets our names mixed up, as well as the subjects he's supposed to be teaching. At out last lesson, instead of maths, he taught us geography!'

'More fun than maths,' said Bina.

'Yes, but there's a new teacher this year. She's very young, they say, just out of college. I wonder what she'll be like.'

Bina walked faster and Sonu had some trouble keeping up with them. She was excited about the new school and the prospect of different surroundings. She had seldom been outside her own village, with its small school and single ration shop. The day's routine never varied—helping her mother in the fields or with household tasks like fetching water from the spring or cutting grass and fodder for the cattle. Her father, who was a soldier, used to be away for nine months in the year and Sonu was still too small for the heavier tasks.

As they neared Nauti village, they were joined by other children coming from different directions. Even where there were no major roads, the mountains were full of little lanes and short cuts. Like a game of snakes and ladders, these narrow paths zigzagged around the hills and villages, cutting through fields and crossing narrow ravines until they came together to form a fairly busy road along which mules, cattle and goats joined the throng.

Nauti was a fairly large village, and from there a broader but dustier road started for Tehri. There was a small bus, several trucks and (for part of the way) a road roller. The road hadn't been completed because the heavy diesel roller couldn't take the steep climb to Nauti. It stood on the roadside halfway up the road from Tehri.

Prakash knew almost everyone in the area, and exchanged greetings and gossip with other children as well as with muleteers, bus drivers, milkmen and labourers working on the road. He loved telling everyone the time, even if they weren't interested.

'It's nine o'clock,' he would announce, glancing at his wrist. 'Isn't your bus leaving today?'

'Off with you!' the bus driver would respond, 'I'll leave when I'm ready.'

As the children approached Nauti, the small flat school buildings came into view on the outskirts of the village, fringed with a line of long-leaved pines. A small crowd had assembled on the playing field. Something unusual seemed to have happened. Prakash ran forward to see what it was all about. Bina and Sonu stood aside, waiting in a patch of sunlight near the boundary wall.

Prakash soon came running back to them. He was bubbling over with excitement.

'It's Mr Mani!' he gasped. 'He's disappeared! People are saying a leopard must have carried him off!'

2

Mr Mani wasn't really old. He was about fifty-five and was expected to retire soon. But for the children, adults over forty seemed ancient! And Mr Mani had always been a bit absent-minded, even as a young man.

He had gone out for his early morning walk, saying he'd be back by eight o'clock, in time to have his breakfast and be ready for class. He wasn't married, but his sister and her husband stayed with him. When it was past nine o'clock his sister presumed he'd stopped at a neighbour's house for breakfast (he loved tucking into other people's breakfast) and that he had gone on to school from there. But when the school bell rang at ten o'clock, and everyone but Mr Mani was present, questions were asked and guesses were made.

No one had seen him return from his walk and enquiries made in the village showed that he had not stopped at anyone's house. For Mr Mani to disappear was puzzling; for him to disappear without his breakfast was extraordinary.

Then a milkman returning from the next village said he had seen a leopard sitting on a rock on the outskirts of the pine forest. There had been talk of a cattle-killer in the valley, of leopards and other animals being displaced by the construction of a dam. But as yet no one had heard of a leopard attacking a man. Could Mr Mani have been its first victim? Someone found a strip of red cloth entangled in a blackberry bush and went running through the village showing it to everyone. Mr Mani had been known to wear red pyjamas. Surely, he had been seized and eaten! But where were his remains? And why had he been in his pyjamas?

Meanwhile, Bina and Sonu and the rest of the children had followed their teachers into the school playground. Feeling a little lost, Bina looked around for Prakash. She found herself facing a dark slender young woman wearing spectacles, who must have been in her early twenties—just a little too old to be another student. She had a kind expressive face and she seemed a little concerned by all that had been happening.

Bina noticed that she had lovely hands; it was obvious that the new teacher hadn't milked cows or worked in the fields!

'You must be new here,' said the teacher, smiling at Bina. 'And is this your little brother?'

'Yes, we've come from Koli village. We were at school there.'

'It's a long walk from Koli. You didn't see any leopards, did you? Well, I'm new too. Are you in the sixth class?'

'Sonu is in the third class. I'm in the sixth class.'

'Then I'm your new teacher. My name is Tania Ramola. Come along, let's see if we can settle down in our classroom.'

Mr Mani turned up at twelve o'clock, wondering what all the fuss was about. No, he snapped, he had not been attacked by a leopard; and yes, he had lost his pyjamas and would someone kindly return them to him?

'How did you lose your pyjamas, Sir?' asked Prakash.

'They were blown off the washing line!' snapped Mr Mani.

After much questioning, Mr Mani admitted that he had gone further than he had intended, and that he had lost his way coming back. He had been a bit upset because the new teacher, a slip of a girl, had been given charge of the sixth grade, while he was still with the fifth grade, along with that troublesome boy Prakash, who kept on reminding him of the time! The headmaster had explained that as Mr Mani was due to retire at the end of the year, the school did not wish to burden him with a senior class. But Mr Mani looked upon the whole thing as a plot to get rid of him. He glowered at Miss Ramola whenever he passed her. And when she smiled back at him, he looked the other way!

Mr Mani had been getting even more absent-minded of late—putting on his shoes without his socks, wearing his homespun waistcoat inside out, mixing up people's names and, of course, eating other people's lunches and dinners. His sister had made a special mutton broth (*pai*) for the postmaster, who was down with flu and had asked Mr Mani to take it over in a thermos. When the postmaster opened the thermos, he found only a few drops of broth at the bottom—Mr Mani had drunk the rest somewhere along the way.

When sometimes Mr Mani spoke of his coming retirement, it was to describe his plans for the small field he owned just behind the house. Right now, it was full of potatoes, which did not require much looking after; but he had plans for growing dahlias, roses, French beans and other fruits and flowers.

The next time he visited Tehri, he promised himself he would buy some dahlia bulbs and rose cuttings. The monsoon season would be a good time to put them down. And meanwhile, his potatoes were still flourishing.

3

Bina enjoyed her first day at the new school. She felt at ease with Miss Ramola, as did most of the boys and girls in her class. Tania Ramola had been to distant towns such as Delhi and Lucknow—places they had only read about—and it was said that she had a brother who was a pilot and flew planes all over the world. Perhaps he'd fly over Nauti some day!

Most of the children had, of course, seen planes flying overhead, but none of them had seen a ship, and only a few had been in a train. Tehri mountain was far from the railway and hundreds of miles from the sea. But they all knew about the big dam that was being built in Tehri, just forty miles away.

Bina, Sonu and Prakash had company for part of the way home, but gradually the other children went off in different directions. Once they had crossed the stream, they were on their own again.

It was a steep climb all the way back to their village. Prakash had a supply of peanuts, which he shared with Bina and Sonu, and they quenched their thirst at a small spring.

When they were less than a mile from home, they met a postman who had finished his round of the villages in the area and was now returning to Nauti.

'Don't waste time along the way,' he told them. 'Try to get home before dark.'

'What's the hurry?' asked Prakash, glancing at his watch. 'It's only five o'clock.'

'There's a leopard around. I saw it this morning, not far from the stream. No one is sure how it got here. So don't take any chances. Get home early.'

'So there really is a leopard,' said Sonu.

They took his advice and walked faster, and Sonu forgot to complain about his aching feet.

They were home well before sunset.

There was a smell of cooking in the air and they were hungry.

'Cabbage and roti,' said Prakash gloomily. 'But I could eat anything today.' He stopped outside his small slate-roofed house, and Bina and Sonu waved him goodbye, then carried on across a couple of ploughed fields until they reached their small stone house.

'Stuffed tomatoes,' said Sonu, sniffing just outside the front door.

'And lemon pickle,' said Bina, who had helped cut, sun and salt the lemons a month ago.

Their mother was lighting the kitchen stove. They greeted her with great hugs and demands for an immediate dinner. She was a good cook who could make even the simplest of dishes taste delicious. Her favourite saying was, 'Homemade *pai* is better than chicken soup in Delhi,' and Bina and Sonu had to agree.

Electricity had yet to reach their village, and they took their meal by the light of a kerosene lamp. After the meal, Sonu settled down to do a little homework, while Bina stepped outside to look at the stars.

Across the fields, someone was playing a flute. 'It must be Prakash,' thought Bina. 'He always breaks off on the high notes.' But the flute music was simple and appealing, and she began singing softly to herself in the dark.

4

Mr Mani was having trouble with the porcupines. They had been getting into his garden at night and digging up and eating his potatoes. From his bedroom window—left open, now that the mild-April weather had arrived—he could hear them enjoying the vegetables he had worked hard to grow. Scrunch, scrunch! *Katar, katar*, their sharp teeth sliced through the largest and juiciest of potatoes. For Mr Mani it was as though they were biting through his own flesh. The sound of them digging industriously as they rooted up those healthy, leafy plants, made him tremble with rage and indignation. The unfairness of it all!

Yes, Mr Mani hated porcupines. He prayed for their destruction, their removal from the face of the earth. But, as his friends were quick to point out, 'Bhagwan protected porcupines too,' and in any case you could never see the creatures or catch them, they are completely nocturnal.

Mr Mani got out of bed every night, torch in one hand, a stout stick in the other, but as soon as he stepped into the garden the crunching and digging stopped and he was greeted by the most infuriating of silences. He would grope around in the dark, swinging wildly with the stick, but not a single porcupine was to be seen or heard. As soon as he was back in bed—the sounds would start all over again. Scrunch, scrunch, *katar, katar*...

Mr Mani came to his class tired and dishevelled, with dark circles beneath his eyes and a permanent frown on his face. It took some time for his pupils to discover the reason for his misery, but when they did, they felt sorry for their teacher and took to discussing ways and means of saving his potatoes from the porcupines.

It was Prakash who came up with the idea of a moat or water ditch. 'Porcupines don't like water,' he said knowledgeably.

'How do you know?' asked one of his friends.

'Throw water on one and see how it runs! They don't like getting their quills wet.'

There was no one who could disprove Prakash's theory, and the class fell in with the idea of building a moat, especially as it meant getting most of the day off.

'Anything to make Mr Mani happy,' said the headmaster, and the rest of the school watched with envy as the pupils of class five, armed with spades and shovels collected from all parts of the village, took up their positions around Mr Mani's potato field and began digging a ditch.

By evening, the moat was ready, but it was still dry and the porcupines got in again that night and had a great feast.

'At this rate,' said Mr Mani gloomily 'there won't be any potatoes left to save.'

But next day Prakash and the other boys and girls managed to divert the water from a stream that flowed past the village. They had the satisfaction of watching it flow gently into the ditch. Everyone went home in a good mood. By nightfall, the ditch had overflowed, the potato field was flooded, and Mr Mani found himself trapped inside his house. But Prakash and his friends had won the day. The porcupines stayed away that night!

A month had passed, and wild violets, daisies and buttercups now sprinkled the hill slopes, and on her way to school Bina gathered enough to make a little posy. The bunch of flowers fitted easily into an old ink well. Miss Ramola was delighted to find this little display in the middle of her desk.

'Who put these here?' she asked in surprise.

Bina kept quiet, and the rest of the class smiled secretively. After that, they took turns bringing flowers for the classroom.

On her long walks to school and home again, Bina became aware that April was the month of new leaves. The oak leaves were bright green above and silver beneath, and when they rippled in the breeze they were like clouds of silvery green. The path was strewn with old leaves, dry and crackly. Sonu loved kicking them around.

Clouds of white butterflies floated across the stream. Sonu was chasing a butterfly when he stumbled over something dark and repulsive. He was sprawled on the grass. When he got to his feet, he looked down at the remains of a small animal.

'Bina! Prakash! Come quickly!' he shouted.

It was part of a sheep, killed some days earlier by a much larger animal.

'Only a leopard could have done this,' said Prakash.

'Let's get away, then,' said Sonu. 'It might still be around!'

'No, there's nothing left to eat. The leopard will be hunting elsewhere by now. Perhaps it's moved on to the next valley.'

'Still, I'm frightened,' said Sonu. 'There may be more leopards!'

Bina took him by the hand. 'Leopards don't attack humans!' she said.

'They will, if they get a taste for people!' insisted Prakash.

'Well, this one hasn't attacked any people as yet,' said Bina, although she couldn't be sure. Hadn't there been rumours of a leopard attacking some workers near the dam? But she did not want Sonu to feel afraid, so she did not mention the story. All she said was, 'It has probably come here because of all the activity near the dam.'

All the same, they hurried home. And for a few days, whenever they reached the stream, they crossed over very quickly, unwilling to linger too long at that lovely spot.

5

A few days later, a school party was on its way to Tehri to see the new dam that was being built.

Miss Ramola had arranged to take her class, and Mr Mani, not wishing to be left out, insisted on taking his class as well. This meant there were about fifty boys and girls taking part in the outing. The little bus could only take thirty. A friendly truck driver agreed to take some children if they were prepared to sit on sacks of potatoes. And Prakash persuaded the owner of the diesel roller to turn it around and head it back to Tehri—with him and a couple of friends up on the driving seat.

Prakash's small group set off at sunrise, as they had to walk some distance in order to reach the stranded road roller. The bus left at 9.00 a.m. with Miss Ramola, her class, Mr Mani and some of his pupils. The truck was to follow later.

It was Bina's first visit to a large town and her first bus ride.

The sharp curves along the winding, downhill road made several children feel sick. The bus driver seemed to be in a tearing hurry. He took them along at rolling, rollicking speed, which made Bina feel quite giddy. She rested her head on her arms and refused to look out of the window. Hairpin bends and cliff edges, pine forests and snowcapped peaks, all swept past her, but she felt too ill to want to look at anything. It was just as well—those sudden drops, hundreds of feet to the valley below, were quite frightening. Bina began to wish that she hadn't come—or that she had joined Prakash on the road roller instead!

Miss Ramola and Mr Mani didn't seem to notice the lurching and groaning of the old bus. They had made this journey many times. They were busy arguing about the advantages and disadvantages of large dams—an argument that was to continue on and off for much of the day; sometimes in Hindi, sometimes in English, sometimes in the local dialect!

Meanwhile, Prakash and his friends had reached the roller. The driver hadn't turned up, but they managed to reverse it and get it going in the direction of Tehri. They were soon overtaken by both the bus and the truck but kept moving along at a steady chug. Prakash spotted Bina at the window of the bus and waved cheerfully. She responded feebly.

Bina felt better when the road levelled out near Tehri. As they crossed an old bridge over the wide river, they were startled by a loud bang which made the bus shudder. A cloud of dust rose above the town.

'They're blasting the mountain,' said Miss Ramola.

'End of a mountain,' said Mr Mani mournfully.

While they were drinking cups of tea at the bus stop, waiting for the potato truck and the road roller, Miss Ramola and Mr Mani continued their argument about the dam. Miss Ramola maintained that it would bring electric power and water for irrigation to large areas of the country, including the surrounding area. Mr Mani declared that it was a menace, as it was situated in an earthquake zone. There would be a terrible disaster if the dam burst! Bina found it all very confusing. And what about the animals in the area, she wondered, what would happen to them?

The argument was becoming quite heated when the potato truck arrived. There was no sign of the road roller, so it was decided that Mr Mani should wait for Prakash and his friends while Miss Ramola's group went ahead.

Some eight or nine miles before Tehri the road roller had broken down, and Prakash and his friends were forced to walk. They had not gone far, however, when a mule train came along—five or six mules that had been delivering sacks of grain in Nauti. A boy rode on the first mule, but the others had no loads.

'Can you give us a ride to Tehri?' called Prakash.

'Make yourselves comfortable,' said the boy.

There were no saddles, only gunny sacks strapped on to the mules with rope. They had a rough but jolly ride down to the Tehri bus stop. None of them had ever ridden mules; but they had saved at least an hour on the road.

Looking around the bus stop for the rest of the party, they could find no one from their school. And Mr Mani, who should have been waiting for them, had vanished.

6

Tania Ramola and her group had taken the steep road to the hill above Tehri. Half an hour's climbing brought them to a little plateau which overlooked the town, the river and the dam site.

The earthworks for the dam were only just coming up, but a wide tunnel had been bored through the mountain to divert the river into another channel. Down below, the old town was still spread out across the valley and from a distance it looked quite charming and picturesque.

'Will the whole town be swallowed up by the waters of the dam?' asked Bina.

'Yes, all of it,' said Miss Ramola. 'The clock tower and the old palace. The long bazaar, and the temples, the schools and the jail, and hundreds of houses, for many miles up the valley. All those people will have to go—thousands of them! Of course, they'll be resettled elsewhere.'

'But the town's been here for hundreds of years,' said Bina. 'They were quite happy without the dam, weren't they?'

'I suppose they were. But the dam isn't just for them—it's for the millions who live further downstream, across the plains.'

'And it doesn't matter what happens to this place?'

'The local people will be given new homes, somewhere else.' Miss Ramola found herself on the defensive and decided to change the subject. 'Everyone must be hungry. It's time we had our lunch.'

Bina kept quiet. She didn't think the local people would want to go away. And it was a good thing, she mused, that there was only a small stream and not a big river running past her village. To be uprooted like this—a town and hundreds of villages—and put down somewhere on the hot, dusty plains—seemed to her unbearable.

'Well, I'm glad I don't live in Tehri,' she said.

She did not know it, but all the animals and most of the birds had already left the area. The leopard had been among them.

They walked through the colourful, crowded bazaar, where fruit sellers did business beside silversmiths, and pavement vendors sold everything from umbrellas to glass bangles. Sparrows attacked sacks of grain, monkeys made off with bananas and stray cows and dogs rummaged in refuse bins, but nobody took any notice. Music blared from radios. Buses blew their horns. Sonu bought a whistle to add to the general din, but Miss Ramola told him to put it away. Bina had kept ten rupees aside, and now she used it to buy a cotton head scarf for her mother.

As they were about to enter a small restaurant for a meal, they were joined by Prakash and his companions; but of Mr Mani there was still no sign.

'He must have met one of his relatives,' said Prakash. 'He has relatives everywhere.'

After a simple meal of rice and lentils, they walked the length of the bazaar without seeing Mr Mani. At last, when they were about to give up the search, they saw him emerge from a bylane, a large sack slung over his shoulder.

'Sir, where have you been?' asked Prakash. 'We have been looking for you everywhere.'

On Mr Mani's face was a look of triumph.

'Help me with this bag,' he said breathlessly.

'You've bought more potatoes, Sir,' said Prakash.

'Not potatoes, boy. Dahlia bulbs!'

7

It was dark by the time they were all back in Nauti. Mr Mani had refused to be separated from his sack of dahlia bulbs, and had been forced to sit in the back of the truck with Prakash and most of the boys.

Bina did not feel so ill on the return journey. Going uphill was definitely better than going downhill! But by the time the bus reached Nauti, it was too late for most of the children to walk back to the more distant villages. The boys were put up in different homes, while the girls were given beds in the school verandah.

The night was warm and still. Large moths fluttered around the single bulb that lit the verandah. Counting moths, Sonu soon fell asleep. But Bina stayed awake for some time, listening to the sounds of the night. A nightjar went *tonk-tonk* in the bushes, and somewhere in the forest an owl hooted softly. The sharp call of a barking deer travelled up the valley, from the direction of the stream. Jackals kept howling. It seemed that there were more of them than ever before.

Bina was not the only one to hear the barking deer. The leopard, stretched full length on a rocky ledge, heard it too. It raised its head and then got up slowly. The deer was its natural prey. But there weren't many left, and that was why the leopard, robbed of its forest by the dam, had taken to attacking dogs and cattle near the villages.

As the cry of the barking deer sounded nearer, the leopard left its lookout point and moved swiftly through the shadows towards the stream.

8

In early June, the hills were dry and dusty, and forest fires broke out, destroying shrubs and trees, killing birds and small animals. The resin in the pines made these trees burn more fiercely, and the wind would take sparks from the trees and carry them into the dry grass and leaves, so that new fires would spring up before the old ones had died out. Fortunately, Bina's village was not in the pine belt; the fires did not reach it. But Nauti was surrounded by a fire that raged for three days, and the children had to stay away from school.

And then, towards the end of June, the monsoon rains arrived and there was an end to the forest fires. The monsoon lasts three months and the lower Himalayas are drenched in rain, mist and clouds for the next three months.

The first rain arrived while Bina, Prakash and Sonu were returning home from school. Those first few drops on the dusty path made them cry out with excitement. Then the rain grew heavier and a wonderful aroma rose from the earth.

'The best smell in the world!' exclaimed Bina.

Everything suddenly came to life. The grass, the crops, the trees, the birds. Even the leaves of the trees glistened and looked new.

That first wet weekend, Bina and Sonu helped their mother plant beans, maize and cucumbers. Sometimes, when the rain was very heavy, they had to run indoors. Otherwise they worked in the rain, the soft mud clinging to their bare feet.

Prakash now owned a black dog with one ear up and one ear down. The dog ran around getting in everyone's way, barking at cows, goats, hens and humans, without frightening any of them. Prakash said it was a very clever dog, but no one else seemed to think so. Prakash also said it would protect the village from the leopard, but others said the dog would be the first to be taken—he'd run straight into the jaws of Mr Spots!

In Nauti, Tania Ramola was trying to find a dry spot in the quarters she'd been given. It was an old building and the roof was leaking in several places. Mugs and buckets were scattered about the floor in order to catch the drip.

Mr Mani had dug up all his potatoes and presented them to the friends and neighbours who had given him lunches and dinners. He was having the time of his life, planting dahlia bulbs all over his garden.

'I'll have a field of many-coloured dahlias!' he announced. 'Just wait till the end of August!'

'Watch out for those porcupines,' warned his sister. 'They eat dahlia bulbs too!'

Mr Mani made an inspection tour of his moat, no longer in flood, and found everything in good order. Prakash had done his job well.

Now, when the children crossed the stream, they found that the water level had risen by about a foot. Small cascades had turned into waterfalls. Ferns had sprung up on the banks. Frogs chanted.

Prakash and his dog dashed across the stream. Bina and Sonu followed more cautiously. The current was much stronger now and the water was almost up to their knees. Once they had crossed the stream, they hurried along the path, anxious not to be caught in a sudden downpour.

By the time they reached school, each of them had two or three leeches clinging to their legs. They had to use salt to remove them. The leeches were the most troublesome part of the rainy season. Even the leopard did not like them. It could not lie in the long grass without getting leeches on its paws and face.

One day, when Bina, Prakash and Sonu were about to cross the stream, they heard a low rumble, which grew louder every second. Looking up at the opposite hill, they saw several trees shudder, tilt outwards and begin to fall. Earth and rocks bulged out from the mountain, then came crashing down into the ravine.

'Landslide!' shouted Sonu.

'It has carried away the path,' said Bina. 'Don't go any further.'

There was a tremendous roar as more rocks, trees and bushes fell away and crashed down the hillside.

Prakash's dog, who had gone ahead, came running back, tail between his legs.

They remained rooted to the spot until the rocks had stopped falling and the dust had settled. Birds circled the area, calling wildly. A frightened barking deer ran past them.

'We can't go to school now,' said Prakash. 'There's no way around.'

They turned and trudged home through the gathering mist.

In Koli, Prakash's parents had heard the roar of the landslide. They were setting out in search of the children when they saw them emerge from the mist, waving cheerfully.

9

They had to miss school for another three days, and Bina was afraid they might not be able to take their final exams. Although Prakash was not really troubled by the thought of missing exams, he did not like feeling helpless just because their path had been swept away. So he explored the hillside until he found a goat track going around the mountain. It joined up with another path near Nauti. This made their walk longer by a mile, but Bina did not mind. It was much cooler now that the rains were in full swing.

The only trouble with the new route was that it passed close to the leopard's lair. The animal had made this area its own since being forced to leave the dam area.

One day, Prakash's dog ran ahead of them, barking furiously.

Then he ran back, whimpering.

'He's always running away from something,' observed Sonu. But a minute later he understood the reason for the dog's fear.

They rounded a bend and Sonu saw the leopard standing in their way. They were struck dumb—too terrified to run. It was a strong, sinewy creature. A low growl rose from its throat. It seemed ready to spring.

They stood perfectly still, afraid to move or say a word. And the leopard must have been equally surprised. It stared at them for a few seconds, then bounded across the path and into the oak forest.

Sonu was shaking. Bina could hear her heart hammering. Prakash could only stammer: 'Did you see the way he sprang? Wasn't he beautiful?'

He forgot to look at his watch for the rest of the day.

A few days later, Sonu stopped and pointed to a large outcrop of rock on the next hill.

The leopard stood far above them, outlined against the sky. It looked strong, majestic. Standing beside it were two young cubs.

'Look at those little ones!' exclaimed Sonu.

'So it's a female, not a male,' said Prakash.

'That's why she was killing so often,' said Bina. 'She had to feed her cubs too.'

They remained still for several minutes, gazing up at the leopard and her cubs. The leopard family took no notice of them.

'She knows we are here,' said Prakash, 'but she doesn't care. She knows we won't harm them.'

'We are cubs too!' said Sonu.

'Yes,' said Bina. 'And there's still plenty of space for all of us. Even when the dam is ready there will still be room for leopards and humans.'

10

The school exams were over. The rains were nearly over too. The landslide had been cleared, and Bina, Prakash and Sonu were once again crossing the stream.

There was a chill in the air, for it was the end of September.

Prakash had learnt to play the flute quite well, and he played on the way to school and then again on the way home. As a result, he did not look at his watch so often.

One morning, they found a small crowd in front of Mr Mani's house.

'What could have happened?' wondered Bina. 'I hope he hasn't got lost again.'

'Maybe he's sick,' said Sonu.

'Maybe it's the porcupines,' said Prakash.

But it was none of these things.

Mr Mani's first dahlia was in bloom, and half the village had turned out to look at it! It was a huge red double dahlia, so heavy that it had to be supported with sticks. No one had ever seen such a magnificent flower!

Mr Mani was a happy man. And his mood only improved over the coming week, as more and more dahlias flowered—crimson, yellow, purple, mauve, white—button dahlias, pompom dahlias, spotted dahlias, striped dahlias… Mr Mani had them all! A dahlia even turned up on Tania Romola's desk—he got on quite well with her now—and another brightened up the headmaster's study.

A week later, on their way home—it was almost the last day of the school term—Bina, Prakash and Sonu were talking about what they might do when they grew up.

'I think I'll become a teacher,' said Bina. 'I'll teach children about animals and birds, and trees and flowers.'

'Better than maths!' said Prakash.

'I'll be a pilot,' said Sonu. 'I want to fly a plane like Miss Ramola's brother.'

'And what about you, Prakash?' asked Bina.

Prakash just smiled and said, 'Maybe I'll be a flute player,' and he put the flute to he lips and played a sweet melody.

'Well, the world needs flute players too,' said Bina as they fell into step beside him.

The leopard had been stalking a barking deer. She paused when she heard the flute and the voices of the children. Her own young ones were growing quickly, but the girl and the two boys did not look much older.

They had started singing their favourite song again.

Five more miles to go!
We climb through rain and snow.
A river to cross…
A mountain to pass…
Now we've four more miles to go!

The leopard waited until they had passed, before returning to the trail of the barking deer.

THE LONG DAY

Suraj was awakened by the sound of his mother busying herself in the kitchen. He lay in bed, looking through the open window at the sky getting lighter and the dawn pushing its way into the room. He knew there was something important about this new day, but for some time he couldn't remember what it was. Then, as the room cleared, so did his mind. His school report would be arriving in the post.

Suraj knew he had failed. The class teacher had told him so. But his mother would only know of it when she read the report, and Suraj did not want to be in the house when she received it. He was sure it would be arriving today. So he had told his mother that he would be having his midday meal with his friend Somi—who wasn't even in town at the moment—and would be home only for the evening meal. By that time, he hoped, his mother would have recovered from the shock. He was glad his father was away on tour.

He slipped out of bed and went to the kitchen. His mother was surprised to see him up so early.

'I'm going for a walk, Ma,' he said, 'and then I'll go on to Somi's house.'

'Well, have your bath first and put something in your stomach.'

Suraj went to the tap in the courtyard and took a quick bath. He put on a clean shirt and shorts. Carelessly, he brushed his thick, curly hair, knowing he couldn't bring much order to its wildness. Then he gulped down a glass of milk and hurried out of the house. The postman wouldn't arrive for a couple of hours, but Suraj felt that the earlier his start the better. His mother was surprised and pleased to see him up and about so early.

Suraj was out on the maidaan and still the sun had not risen. The maidaan was an open area of grass, about a hundred square metres, and from the middle of it could be seen the mountains, range upon range of them, stepping into the sky. A game of football was in progress, and one of the players called out to Suraj to join them. Suraj said he wouldn't play for more than ten minutes because he had some business to attend to; he kicked off his chappals and ran barefoot after the ball. Everyone was playing barefoot. It was an informal game, and the players were of all ages and sizes, from bearded Sikhs to small boys of six or seven. Suraj ran all over the place without actually touching the ball—he wasn't too good at football—and finally got into a scramble before the goal, fell and scratched his knee. He retired from the game even sooner than he had intended.

The scratch wasn't bad but there was some blood on his knee. He wiped it clean with his handkerchief and limped off the maidaan. He went in the direction of the railway station, but not through the bazaar. He went by way of the canal, which came from the foot of the nearest mountain, flowed through the town and down to the river. Beside the canal were the washerwomen, scrubbing and beating out clothes on the stone banks.

The canal was only a metre wide but, due to recent rain, the current was swift and noisy. Suraj stood on the bank, watching the rush of water. There was an inlet at one place, and there some children were bathing, and some were rushing up and down the bank, wearing nothing at all, shouting to each other in high spirits. Suraj felt like taking a dip too, but he did not know any of the children there; most of them were from very poor families. Hands in pockets, he walked along the canal banks.

The sun had risen and was shining through the branches of the trees that lined the road. The leaves made shadowy patterns on the ground. Suraj tried hard not to think of his school report, but he knew that at any moment now the postman would be handing over a long brown envelope to his mother. He tried to imagine his mother's expression when she read the report; but the more he tried to picture her face, the more certain he was that, on knowing his result, she would show no expression at all. And having no expression on her face was much worse than having one.

Suraj heard the whistle of a train, and knew he was not far from the station. He cut through a field, climbed a hillock and ran down the slope until he was near the railway tracks. Here came the train, screeching and puffing; in the distance, a big black beetle, and then, when the carriages swung into sight, a centipede.

Suraj stood a good twenty metres away from the lines, on the slope of the hill. As the train passed, he pulled the handkerchief off his knee and began to wave it furiously. There was something about passing trains that filled him with awe and excitement. All those passengers, with mysterious lives and mysterious destinations, were people he wanted to know, people whose mysteries he wanted to unfold. He had been in a train recently, when his parents had taken him to bathe in the sacred river, Ganga, at Haridwar. He wished he could be in a train now; or, better still, be an engine driver, with no more books and teachers and school reports. He did not know of any thirteen-year-old engine-drivers, but he saw himself driving the engine, shouting orders to the stoker; it made him feel powerful to imagine being in control of a mighty steam-engine.

Someone—another boy—returned his wave, and the two waved at each other for a few seconds, and then the train had passed, its smoke spiralling backwards.

Suraj felt a little lonely now. Somehow, the passing of the train left him with a feeling of being alone in a wide, empty world. He was feeling hungry too. He went back to the field where he had seen some lichi trees, climbed into one of them and began plucking and peeling and eating the juicy red-skinned fruit. No one seemed to own the lichi trees because, although a dog appeared below and began barking, no one else showed up. Suraj kept spitting lichi seeds at the dog, who kept barking at him. Eventually, the dog lost interest and slunk off.

Suraj began to feel drowsy in the afternoon heat. The lichi trees offered a lot of shade below, so he came down from the tree and sat on the grass, his back resting against the tree-trunk. A mynah-bird came hopping up to his feet and looked at him curiously, its head tilted to one side.

Insects kept buzzing around Suraj. He swiped at them once or twice, but then couldn't make the effort to keep swiping. He opened his shirt buttons. The air was very hot, very still; the only sound was the faint buzzing of the insects. His head fell forward on his chest.

He opened his eyes to find himself being shaken, and looked up into the round, cheerful face of his friend Ranji.

'What are you doing, sleeping here?' asked Ranji, who was a couple of years younger than Suraj. 'Have you run away from home?'

'Not yet,' said Suraj. 'And what are you doing here?'

'Came for lichis.'

'So did I.'

They sat together for a while and talked and ate lichis. Then Ranji suggested that they visit the bazaar to eat pakoras.

'I haven't any money,' said Suraj.

'That doesn't matter,' said Ranji, who always seemed to be in funds. 'I have two rupees.'

So they walked to the bazaar. They crossed the field, walked back past the canal, skirted the maidaan, came to the clock tower and entered the bazaar.

The evening crowd had just begun to fill the road, and there was a lot of bustle and noise: the street-vendors called their wares in high, strident voices; children shouted and women bargained. There was a medley of smells and aromas coming from the little restaurants and sweet shops, and a mishmash of colours in the bangle and kite shops. Suraj and Ranji ate their pakoras, felt thirsty and gazed at the rows and rows of coloured bottles at the cold drinks shop, where at least ten varieties of sweet, sticky, fizzy drinks were available. But they had already finished the two rupees, so there was nothing for them to do but quench their thirst at the municipal tap.

Afterwards they wandered down the crowded street, examining the shop-fronts, commenting on the passers-by, and every now and then greeting some friend or acquaintance. Darkness came on suddenly, and then the bazaar was lit up, the big shops with bright electric and neon lights, the street vendors with oil lamps. The bazaar at night was even more exciting than during the day.

They traversed the bazaar from end to end, and when they were at the clock tower again, Ranji said he had to go home, and left Suraj. It was nearing Suraj's dinnertime and so, unwillingly, he too turned homewards. He did not want it to seem like he was deliberately staying out late because of the school report.

The lights were on in the front room when he got home. He waited outside, secure in the darkness of the verandah, watching the lighted room. His mother would be waiting for him, she would probably have the report in her hand or on the kitchen shelf, and she would have lots and lots of questions to ask him. All the cares of the world seemed to descend on Suraj as he crept into the house.

'You're late,' said his mother. 'Come and have your food.'

Suraj said nothing, but removed his shoes outside the kitchen and sat down cross-legged on the kitchen floor, which was where he took his meals. He was tired and hungry. He no longer cared about anything.

'One of your class-fellows dropped in,' said his mother. 'He said your reports were sent out today. They'll arrive tomorrow.'

Tomorrow! Suraj felt a great surge of relief.

But then, just as suddenly, his spirits fell again.

Tomorrow…a further postponement of the dread moment, another night and another morning something would have to be done about it!

'Ma,' he said abruptly. 'Somi has asked me to his house again tomorrow.'

'I don't know how his mother puts up with you so often,' said Suraj's mother.

Suraj lay awake in bed, planning the morrow's activities: a game of cricket or football on the maidaan; perhaps a dip in the canal; a half-hour watching the trains thunder past; and in the evening an hour in the bazaar, among the kites, balloons, rose-coloured fizzy drinks and round dripping syrupy sweets…

Perhaps, in the morning, he could persuade his mother to give him two or three rupees… It would be his last pocketmoney for quite some time.

BE PREPARED

I was a Boy Scout once, although I couldn't tell a slip knot from a granny knot, nor a reef knot from a thief knot. I did know that a thief knot was to be used to tie up a thief, should you happen to catch one. I have never caught a thief—and wouldn't know what to do with one since I can't tie the right knot. I'd just let him go with a warning, I suppose. And tell him to become a Boy Scout.

'Be prepared!' That's the Boy Scout motto. And it is a good one, too. But I never seem to be well prepared for anything, be it an exam or a journey or the roof blowing off my room. I get halfway through a speech and then forget what I have to say next. Or I make a new suit to attend a friend's wedding, and then turn up in my pyjamas.

So, how did I, the most impractical of boys, survive as a Boy Scout?

Well, it seems a rumour had gone around the junior school (I was still a junior then) that I was a good cook. I had never cooked anything in my life, but of course I had spent a lot of time in the tuck shop making suggestions and advising Chimpu, who ran the shop, encouraging him to make more and better samosas, jalebis, tikkis and pakoras. For my unwanted advice, he would favour me with an occasional free samosa. So, naturally, I looked upon him as a friend and benefactor. With this qualification, I was given a cookery badge and put in charge of our troop's supply of rations.

There were about twenty of us in our troop. During the summer break, our Scoutmaster, Mr Oliver, took us on a camping expedition to Taradevi, a temple-crowned mountain a few miles outside Shimla. That first night we were put to work, peeling potatoes, skinning onions, shelling peas and pounding masalas. These various ingredients being ready, I was asked, as the troop cookery expert, what should be done with them.

'Put everything in that big degchi,' I ordered. 'Pour half a tin of ghee over the lot. Add some nettle leaves, and cook for half an hour.'

When this was done, everyone had a taste, but the general opinion was that the dish lacked something. 'More salt,' I suggested. More salt was added. It still lacked something. 'Add a cup of sugar,' I ordered. Sugar was added to the concoction, but it still lacked something.

'We forgot to add tomatoes,' said one of the Scouts.

'Never mind,' I said. 'We have tomato sauce. Add a bottle of tomato sauce!'

'How about some vinegar?' suggested another boy.

'Just the thing,' I said. 'Add a cup of vinegar!'

'Now it's too sour,' said one of the tasters.

'What jam did we bring?' I asked.

'Gooseberry jam.'

'Just the thing. Empty the bottle!'

The dish was a great success. Everyone enjoyed it, including Mr Oliver, who had no idea what had gone into it.

'What's this called?' he asked.

'It's an all-Indian sweet-and-sour jam-potato curry,' I ventured.

'For short, just call it Bond bhujjia,' said one of the boys. I had earned my cookery badge!

Poor Mr Oliver; he wasn't really cut out to be a Scoutmaster, any more than I was meant to be a Scout.

The following day, he told us he would give us a lesson in tracking. Taking a half-hour start, he walked into the forest, leaving behind him a trail of broken twigs, chicken feathers, pine cones and chestnuts. We were to follow the trail until we found him.

Unfortunately, we were not very good trackers. We did follow Mr Oliver's trail some way into the forest, but then we were distracted by a pool of clear water. It looked very inviting. Abandoning our uniforms, we jumped into the pool and had a great time romping about or just lying on its grassy banks and enjoying the sunshine. Many hours later, feeling hungry, we returned to our campsite and set about preparing the evening meal. It was Bond bhujjia again, but with a few variations.

It was growing dark, and we were beginning to worry about Mr Oliver's whereabouts when he limped into the camp, assisted by a couple of local villagers. Having waited for us at the far end of the forest for a couple of hours, he had decided to return by following his own trail, but in the gathering gloom, he was soon lost. Village folk returning home from the temple took charge and escorted him back to the camp. He was very angry and made us return all our good conduct and other badges, which he stuffed into his haversack. I had to give up my cookery badge.

An hour later, when we were all preparing to get into our sleeping bags for the night, Mr Oliver called out, 'Where's dinner?'

'We've had ours,' said one of the boys. 'Everything is finished, Sir.'

'Where's Bond? He's supposed to be the cook. Bond, get up and make me an omelette.'

'I can't, Sir.'

'Why not?'

'You have my badge. Not allowed to cook without it. Scout rule, Sir.'

'I've never heard of such a rule. But you can take your badges, all of you. We return to school tomorrow.'

Mr Oliver returned to his tent in a huff.

But I relented and made him a grand omelette, garnishing it with dandelion leaves and a chilli.

'Never had such an omelette before,' confessed Mr Oliver.

'Would you like another, Sir?'

'Tomorrow, Bond, tomorrow. We'll breakfast early tomorrow.'

But we had to break up our camp before we could do that because in the early hours of the next morning, a bear strayed into our camp, entered the tent where our stores were kept, and created havoc with all our provisions, even rolling our biggest degchi down the hillside.

In the confusion and uproar that followed, the bear entered Mr Oliver's tent (our Scoutmaster was already outside, fortunately) and came out entangled in his dressing gown. It then made off towards the forest, a comical sight in its borrowed clothes.

And though we were a troop of brave little Scouts, we thought it better to let the bear keep the gown.

THE FOUR FEATHERS

Our school dormitory was a very long room with about thirty beds, fifteen on either side of the room. This was good for pillow fights. Class five would take on class eight (the two senior classes in our prep school) and there would be plenty of space for leaping, struggling small boys, pillows and feathers flying, until there was a cry of 'Here comes Fishy!' or 'Here comes Olly!' and either Mr Fisher, the headmaster, or Mr Oliver, the senior master, would come striding in, cane in hand, to put an end to the general mayhem. Pillow fights were allowed, up to a point; nobody got hurt. But parents sometimes complained if, at the end of the term, a boy came home with a pillow devoid of cotton-wool or feathers.

In that last year at prep school in Shimla, there were four of us who were close friends—Bimal, whose home was in Bombay; Riaz, who came from Lahore; Brian, who hailed from Vellore; and your narrator, who lived wherever his father (then in the Air Force) was posted.

We called ourselves 'four feathers'—the feathers signifying that we were companions in adventure, comrades in arms, knights of the round table, etc. Bimal adopted a peacock's feather as his emblem; he was always a bit showy. Riaz chose a falcon's feather—although we couldn't find one. Brian and I were at first offered crows or *murghi* feathers, but we protested vigorously and threatened a walk out. Finally, I settled for a parrot's feather (taken from Mr Fisher's pet parrot), and Brian found a woodpecker's, which suited him, as he was always knocking things about.

Bimal was all thin legs and arms, so light and frisky that at times he seemed to be walking on air. We called him 'Bambi', after the delicate little deer in the Disney film. Riaz, on the other hand, was a sturdy boy, good at games but not very studious; but always good natured and smiling. Brian was a dark, good-looking boy from the south; he was just a little spoilt—hated being given out in a cricket match and would refuse to leave the crease! But he was affectionate and a loyal friend. I was the 'scribe'—good at inventing stories in order to get out of scrapes—but hopeless at sums, my highest marks being 22 out of 100.

On Sunday afternoons, when there were no classes or organized games, we were allowed to roam about on the hillside below the school. The four feathers would laze about on the short summer grass, sharing the occasional food parcel from home, reading comics (sometimes a book) and making plans for the long winter holidays. My father, who collected everything from stamps to sea shells to butterflies, had given me a butterfly net and urged me to try and catch a rare species which, he said, was found only near Chotta Shimla. He described it as a large purple butterfly with yellow and black borders on its wings. A 'Purple Emperor', I think it was called. As I wasn't very good at identifying butterflies, I would chase anything that happened to flit across the school grounds, usually ending up with common 'Red Admirals', 'Clouded Yellows', or 'Cabbage Whites'. But the 'Purple Emperor'—that rare specimen being sought by collectors the world over—proved elusive. I would have to seek my fortune in some other line of endeavour.

One day, scrambling about among the rocks and thorny

bushes below the school, I almost fell over a small bundle lying in the shade of a young spruce tree. On taking a closer look, I discovered that the bundle was really a baby, wrapped up in a tattered old blanket.

'Feathers, feathers!' I called, 'Come here and look. A baby has been left here!'

The feathers joined me, and we all stared down at the infant, who was fast asleep.

'Who would leave a baby on the hillside?' asked Bimal of no one in particular.

'Someone who doesn't want it,' said Brian.

'And hoped some good people would come along and keep it,' said Riaz.

'A panther might have come along instead,' I said. 'Can't leave it here.'

'Well, we'll just have to adopt it,' said Bimal.

'We can't adopt a baby,' said Brian.

'Why not?'

'We have to be married.'

'We don't.'

'Not us, you dope. The grown-ups who adopt babies.'

'Well, we can't just leave it here for grown-ups to come along,' I said.

'We don't even know if it's a boy or a girl,' said Riaz.

'Makes no difference. A baby is a baby. Let's take it back to school.'

'And keep it in the dormitory?'

'Of course not. Who's going to feed it? Babies need milk. We'll hand it over to Mrs Fisher. She doesn't have a baby.'

'Maybe she doesn't want one. Look, it's beginning to cry. Let's hurry!'

Riaz picked up the wide-awake and crying baby and gave it to Bimal, who gave it to Brian, who gave it to me. The four feathers marched up the hill to school with the very noisy baby.

'Now it has done potty in the blanket,' I complained, 'and some of it is on my shirt.'

'Never mind,' said Bimal. 'It's for a good cause. You're a Boy Scout, remember. You're supposed to help people in distress.'

The headmaster and his wife were in their drawing room, enjoying their afternoon tea and cakes. We trudged in, and Bimal announced, 'We've got something for Mrs Fisher.'

Mrs Fisher took a look at the bundle in my arms and let out a shriek. 'What have you brought here, Bond?'

'A baby, ma'am. I think it's a girl. Do you want to adopt it?'

Mrs Fisher threw up her arms in consternation and turned to her husband. 'What are we to do, Frank? These boys are impossible. They've picked up someone's child!'

'We'll have to inform the police,' said Mr Fisher, reaching for the telephone, 'we can't have lost babies in the school.'

Just then, there was a commotion outside, and a wild-eyed woman, her clothes dishevelled, entered at the front door accompanied by several men-folk from one of the villages. She ran towards us, crying out, 'My baby, my baby! *Mera bachcha*! You've stolen my baby!'

'We found it on the hillside,' I stammered.

'That's right,' said Brian. 'Finders keepers!'

'Quiet, Adams,' said Mr Fisher, holding up his hand for order and addressing the villagers in a friendly manner. 'These boys found the baby alone on the hillside and brought it here before—before—'

'Before the hyaenas got it,' I put in.

'Quite right, Bond. And why did you leave your child

alone?' he asked the woman.

'I put her down for five minutes so that I could climb the plum tree and collect plums. When I came down, the baby was gone! But I could hear it crying up on the hill. I called the men-folk and we came here looking for it.'

'Well, here's your baby,' I said, thrusting it into her arms. By then, I was glad to be rid of it! 'Look after it properly in the future.'

'Kidnapper!' she screamed at me.

Mr Fisher succeeded in mollifying the villagers. 'These boys are good Scouts,' he told them. 'It's their business to help people.'

'Scout Law Number Three, Sir,' I added. 'To be useful and helpful.'

And then the headmaster turned the tables on the villagers. 'By the way, these plum trees belong to the school. So do the peaches and apricots. Now I know why they've been disappearing so fast!'

The villagers, a little chastened, went their way. Mr Fisher reached for his cane. From the way he fondled it, I knew he was itching to use it on our bottoms.

'No, Frank,' said Mrs Fisher, intervening on our behalf. 'It was really very sweet of them to look after that baby. And look at Bond—he's got baby goo all over his clothes.'

'So he has. Go and take a bath, all of you. And what are you grinning about, Bond?' asked Mr Fisher.

'Scout Law Number Eight, Sir. A scout smiles and whistles under all difficulties.'

And so ended the first adventure of the four feathers.

MISS BABCOCK'S BIG TOE

If two people are thrown together for a long time, they can become either close friends or sworn enemies.

Thus it was with Tata and me when we both got down with mumps and had to spend a fortnight together in the school hospital. It wasn't really a hospital—just a five-bed ward in a small cottage on the approach road to our prep school in Chotta Shimla. It was supervised by a retired nurse, an elderly matron called Miss Babcock who was all but stone deaf.

Miss Babcock was an able nurse, but she was a fidgety, fussy person, always dashing about from ward to dispensary, to her own room, and as a result, the boys called her Miss Shuttlecock. As she couldn't hear us, she didn't mind. But her hearing difficulty did create something of a problem—both for her and for her patients. If someone in the ward felt ill late at night, he had to shout or ring a bell—and she heard neither. So someone had to get up and fetch her.

Miss Babcock devised an ingenious method of waking her in an emergency. She tied a long piece of string to the foot of a sick person's bed; then took the other end of the string to her own room where, upon retiring for the night, she tied it to her big toe. A vigorous pull on the string from the sick person, and Miss Babcock would be wide awake!

Now, what could be more tempting than this device? The string was tied to the foot of Tata's bed, and he was a restless fellow, always wanting water, always complaining of aches and pains. Sometimes, out of plain mischief, he would tug that string several times until Miss Babcock arrived with a pill or a glass of water.

'You'll have my toe off by morning,' she complained. 'You don't have to pull quite so hard.'

And what was worse, when Tata did fall asleep, he snored to high heaven and nothing could wake him! I had to lie awake most of the night, listening to his rhythmic snoring. It was like a trumpet tuning up. Or a bullfrog calling to its mate.

Fortunately, a couple of nights later, we were joined in the ward by Bimal, a friend and fellow 'feather', who had also contracted mumps. One night of Tata's snoring, and Bimal resolved to do something about it.

'Wait until he's fast asleep,' said Bimal, 'and then we'll carry his bed outside and leave him on the veranda.' We did more than that. As Tata commenced his nightly imitation of the all-wind instruments in the London Philharmonic Orchestra, we pushed up his bed as gently as possible and carried it out into the garden, putting it down beneath the nearest pine tree.

'It's healthier outside,' said Bimal, justifying our action. 'All this fresh air should cure him.'

Leaving Tata to serenade the stars, we returned to the ward and enjoyed a good night's sleep. So did Miss Babcock.

In fact, no one slept because we were woken by Miss Babcock running around the ward screaming 'Where's Tata there was no sign.' Instead, a large black-faced langur sat at the foot of the bed, showing us its teeth in a grin of disfavor.

'Tata's gone,' gasped Miss Babcock.

'He must be a sleep walker too,' said Bimal.

'Maybe the leopard took him,' I said. Just then, there was a commotion in the shrubbery at the end of the garden, and shouting 'Help, help!' Tata emerged from the bushes, followed by several lithe, long-tailed langurs, merrily, giving chase. Apparently, he'd woken up at the crack of dawn to find his bed surrounded by a gang of inquisitive simians. They had meant no harm; but Tata had panicked, and made a dash for life and liberty, running into the forest instead of into the cottage. We got Tata and his bed back into the ward. Miss Babcock took his temperature and gave him a dose of salts. Oddly enough, in all the excitement, no one asked how Tata and his bed had travelled in the night. And strange to say, he did not snore the following night, so maybe the pine-scented night air really helped. Needless to say, we soon recovered from the mumps, and Miss Babcock's big toe received a well-deserved rest.

READING WAS MY RELIGION

The Royal Air Force (RAF) had undertaken to pay for my schooling, so I was able to continue at the Bishop Cotton School (BCS). Back in Shimla I found a sympathetic soul in Mr Jones, an ex-army Welshman who taught us divinity. He did not have the qualifications to teach us anything else, but I think I learnt more from him than from most of our more qualified staff. He had even got me to read the Bible (King James version) for the classical simplicity of its style.

Mr Jones got on well with small boys, one reason being that he never punished them. Alone among the philistines, he was the only teacher to stand out against corporal punishment. He waged a lone campaign against the custom of caning boys for their misdemeanours, and was thought to be a little eccentric in this respect. He lost his seniority because of his refusal to administer physical punishment.

But there was nothing eccentric about Mr Jones, unless it was the pet pigeon that followed him everywhere and sometimes perched on his bald head. He managed to keep the pigeon (and his cigar) out of the classroom, but his crowded, untidy bachelor quarters reeked of cigar smoke.

He had a passion for the works of Dickens, and when he discovered that I had read *Nicholas Nickleby* and *Sketches by Boz,* he allowed me to look at his set of the *Complete Works,* with the illustrations by Phiz. I launched into *David Copperfield,* which I thoroughly enjoyed, identifying myself with young David, his triumphs and tribulations. After reading *Copperfield* I decided it was a fine thing to be a writer. The seed had already been sown, and although in my imagination I still saw myself as an Arsenal goalkeeper or a Gene Kelly-type tap dancer, I think I knew in my heart that I was best suited to the written word. I was topping the class in essay writing; although I had an aversion to studying the texts that were prescribed for English Literature classes.

Mr Jones, with his socialist, Dickensian viewpoint, had an aversion to P.G. Wodehouse, whose comic novels I greatly enjoyed. He told me that these novels glamorized the most decadent aspects of upper-class English life (which was probably true) and that only recently, during the war (when he was interned in France), Wodehouse had been making propaganda broadcasts on behalf of Germany. This was true, too; although years later when I read the texts of those broadcasts (in *Performing Fled),* they seemed harmless enough.

But Mr Jones did have a point. Wodehouse was hopelessly out of date, for when I went to England after leaving school, I couldn't find anyone remotely resembling a Wodehouse character—except perhaps Ukridge, who was always borrowing money from his friends in order to set up some business or the other. He was universal.

The school library, the Anderson Library, was fairly well-stocked, and it was to be something of a haven for me over the next three years. There were always writers, past or present, to 'discover'—and I still have a tendency to ferret out writers who have been ignored, neglected or forgotten.

After *Copperfield,* the novel that most influenced me was Hugh Walpole's *Fortitude,* an epic account of another young writer in the making. Its opening line still acts as a clarion call when I feel depressed or as though I am getting nowhere: 'Tisn't life that matters! Tis the courage you bring to it.'

Walpole's more ambitious works have been forgotten, but his stories and novels of the macabre are still worth reading—*Mr Perrin and Mr Traill*, *Portrait of a Man with Red Hair*, 'The White Tower' and, of course, *Fortitude*. I returned to it last year and found it was still stirring stuff.

But life wasn't all books. At the age of fifteen, I was at my best as a football goalkeeper, hockey player and athlete. I was also acting in school plays and taking part in debates. I wasn't much of a boxer—the sport I disliked—but I had learnt to use my head to good effect and managed to get myself disqualified by butting the other fellow in the head or midriff. As all games were compulsory, I had to overcome my fear of water and learn to swim a little. Mr Jones taught me to do the breast stroke, saying it was more suited to my temperament than the splash and dash stuff.

The only thing I couldn't do was sing, and although I loved listening to great singers, from Caruso to Gigli, I couldn't sing a note. Our music teacher, Mrs Knight, put me in the school choir because, she said, I looked like a choir boy, all pink and shining in a cassock and surplice, but she forbade me from actually singing. I was to open my mouth with the others, but on no account was I to allow any sound to issue from it.

This took me back to the convent in Mussoorie where I had been given piano lessons, probably at my father's behest. The nun who was teaching me would get so exasperated with my stubborn inability to strike the right chord or play the right notes that she would crack me over the knuckles with a ruler, thus effectively putting to an end any interest I might have had in learning to play a musical instrument. Mr Priestley's violin in prep school, and now Mrs Knight's organ-playing were none too inspiring.

Insensitive though I may have been to high notes and low notes, *diminuendos and crescendos,* I was nevertheless sensitive to sound, such as birdsong, the hum of the breeze playing in tall trees, the rustle of autumn leaves, crickets chirping, water splashing and murmuring brooks, the sea sighing on the sand—all natural sounds, that indicated a certain harmony in the natural world.

Man-made sounds—the roar planes, the blare of horns, the thunder of trucks and engines, the baying of a crowd—are usually ugly, but some gifted humans have risen to create great music. We must not then scorn the also-rans, who come down hard on their organ pedals or emulate cicadas with their violin playing.

Although I was quite popular at BCS, after Omar's departure I did not have many close friends. There was, of course, young A, my junior by two years, who followed me everywhere until I gave in and took him to the pictures in town, or fed him at the tuck shop.

There were just one or two boys who actually read books for pleasure. We tend to think of that era as one when there were no distractions such as television, computer games and the like. But reading has always been a minority pastime. People say children don't read any more. This may be true of the vast majority, but I know many boys and girls who enjoy reading—far more than I encountered when I was a schoolboy. In those days there were comics and the radio and the cinema. I went to the cinema whenever I could, but that did not keep me from reading almost everything that came my way. And so it is today. Book readers are special people, and they will always turn to books as the ultimate pleasure. Those who do not read are the unfortunate ones. There's nothing wrong with them, but they are missing out on one of life's compensations and rewards. A great book is a friend that never lets you down. You can return to it again and again, and the joy first derived from it will still be there.

I think it is fair to say that, when I was a boy, reading was my true religion. It helped me discover my soul.

KOKI PLAYS THE GAME

'There's a cricket match on Saturday, isn't there?' asked Koki.

'That's right,' said Ranji. 'We're playing the Public School team.'

'I might come and watch,' said Koki.

'As you like. It won't be much of a game. We'll beat them easily.'

Ranji's own cricket team was quite different from his school team. It consisted of boys big and small, long and short, from various walks of life. Even Koki, a girl, was allowed honorary membership, and had sometimes been 'twelfth man'—an extra. She knew the game well, and often bowled for Ranji in the mornings when he wanted to practise batting. Only a couple of the teammates could afford to go to private schools like Ranji's; most of them went to the local government school, and two or three had stopped going to school altogether.

There was Bhartu, who delivered newspapers in the mornings; the brothers Mukesh and Rakesh, whose father kept a sweet shop; and a tailor's son, Amir Ali. There was Billy Jones, an Anglo-Indian boy; 'Lumboo', the Tall One; Sitaram, the washerman's son, and several others. And there was also Bhim, who couldn't play at all, but who made a good umpire (when his glasses weren't steamed over) and who accompanied the team wherever it went.

This Saturday they were playing on their 'home' ground, a patch of wasteland behind a new cinema called 'Apsara' ('Heavenly Dancer').

The Public School boys had all arrived first, which was only natural since they lived together in the same boarding school. The members of Ranji's team came from different directions, so it was some time before they had all assembled. Even then, they were two short. But Ranji won the toss and decided to bat, hoping that the missing team members would arrive in time to take their turn at the wicket.

'If Mukesh and Rakesh aren't here in time, we won't have them in the team,' said Ranji sternly.

'Don't sack them,' said Lumboo. 'They always bring us sweets and snacks from their father's shop. We need them in the team even if they don't score any runs.'

'Well, if they turn up *without* refreshments, they'll be sacked,' said Ranji, always ready to be fair.

The two umpires had gone out to set up the stumps—Bhim, on behalf of Ranji's team, and a teacher from the Public School.

'I don't like the look of that teacher,' said Amir Ali.

'Well, we won't take any risks.'

Billy Jones and Lumboo always opened the batting. Lumboo's height helped him to deal with the fast-rising ball. He took the first ball.

The Public School's opening bowler was speedy but inaccurate. This was because he was trying to bowl too fast. His first ball went for a wide, which gave Ranji's team its first run. The second ball wasn't quite so wide, but it was still about a foot from the leg stump. Lumboo took a swipe at it and missed. The third ball pitched halfway down the wicket and kept low. It struck Lumboo on the pads.

'How's that!' shouted the bowler, wicketkeeper and slip-fielders in unison.

The Public School's umpire did not hesitate. Up went his

finger. Lumboo was declared out leg-before-wicket (LBW). Lumboo stood aghast. He looked down at where his feet were placed, then back at his stumps.

'I'm not in front of the wicket,' he complained to no one in particular.

'The umpire's word is law,' said the wicketkeeper.

Lumboo slowly walked back to where his teammates reclined against a pile of bricks.

'I wasn't out!' he protested.

'Never mind,' said Ranji, whose turn it was to bat. 'You'll get your chance when you come on to bowl.'

He walked to the wicket with a confident air, his bat resting on his shoulder. He took guard carefully and, tapping his bat on the ground, faced the bowler. He received a straight ball, fast, and met it on the half-volley, driving it straight back past the bowler. It sped to the boundary, amid delighted cries from Ranji's teammates. Four runs.

The next ball was short, just outside the off stump. Ranji stepped back and square-cut it past point. Another four. There were more cheers, and this time Ranji distinctly heard a girl's voice shouting: 'Good shot, Ranji!'

He looked back to where his teammates were gathered. There was no girl among them. He turned and looked toward the opposite boundary, and there, under the giant cinema hoarding, stood Koki. She waved to him.

Ranji did not wave back. He felt acutely self-conscious. Settling down to face the bowler again, he was aware of two things at once—of the bowler making faces and charging up to bowl, and of Koki standing on the boundary and waiting for him to hit another four.

This loss of concentration caused him to misjudge the next

ball. Instead of playing forward, he played back.

The ball took the edge of his bat and flew straight into the wicketkeeper's gloves.

'How's that!' shouted all the fielders, appealing for a catch.

Ranji did not wait for the umpire—in this case, Bhim, to declare him out. He knew he'd touched the ball. Scowling, he walked back to his team. It was all Koki's fault!

Now, there was a good partnership between Sitaram and Bhartu. Sitaram, who helped his father with the town's washing on Sundays, was in the habit of laying out clothes on a flat stone and pounding them with a stout stick—the method followed by most washermen.

He dealt with the cricket ball in much the same way—clouting it hard, and sending it to various points of the compass. He hit up 25 valuable runs before he was out, caught off a big hit. Bhartu pushed and prodded, merely keeping one end going, until he too was out to an LBW decision. Billy Jones had gone the same way, taking the ball on his pads. No one was happy with the LBW decisions.

'We must have neutral umpires,' said Amir Ali.

'But who wants to be an umpire?' said Ranji. 'We won't find anyone. We'll have to use our own team members—or let the other side provide *both* umpires!'

'Not after today,' said Lumboo.

Meanwhile, Mukesh and Rakesh had arrived, carrying paper bags full of samosas and jalebis. As a result, everyone cheered up. Wickets fell almost as rapidly as the snacks and sweets were consumed. Mukesh and Rakesh, who were the last men in, held out for several overs until Rakesh was given out—LBW! Ranji's team was all out for 87 runs—not really a match-winning score, except on a tricky wicket.

It was the Public School team's turn to bat. One of their opening batsmen was bowled by Lumboo for naught. The other batsman was twice rapped on the pads by balls from Ranji, but his loud appeals for LBW were turned down—by the Public School's umpire, naturally! Muttering to himself, Ranji hurled down a thunderbolt of a ball. It rose sharply and struck the batsman on the hand. Howling with pain, he dropped his bat and wrung his hand. Then he showed everyone a swollen finger and decided to 'retire hurt'.

'There's more than one way of getting them out,' muttered Ranji, as he passed the umpire.

The next two batsmen were good players, not as nervous as the openers. One of them got what might have been a faint tickle to an out-swinger from Lumboo, but he was given the benefit of the doubt by Bhim—who, as umpires went, was as impartial as a star. He showed no favours to his own team, no matter what the other umpire did. It just isn't fair, thought Ranji.

The number three and four batsmen put on 40 runs between them, and by mid-afternoon Ranji's players were feeling tired and hungry. Then three quick wickets fell to Sitaram's spinners. Three wickets remained, and 20 runs were needed by the Public School for victory.

This was when Bhartu, running to take a catch, collided with chubby Mukesh. Both of them went sprawling on the grass, and when they got up, the ball was found lodged at the back of Mukesh's pants. How it got there no one could tell, but after much discussion, the umpires had to agree that it qualified as a catch and the batsman was given out. But Bhartu had to leave the ground with a bleeding nose.

Ranji looked around for a replacement. There was no one in sight except Koki.

'Come and field,' said Ranji brusquely.

Koki needed no persuading. She slipped off her sandals and dashed barefoot on to the field, taking up Bhartu's position near the boundary.

The tail-end batsmen were now swinging at the ball in a desperate attempt to hit the remaining runs. A hard-hit drive sped past Koki and went for four runs. Ranji gave her a hard look. Then the two batsmen got into a muddle while trying to take a quick run, and one of them was run out.

The last man came in. The Public School was 8 runs behind. But a couple of boundaries would take care of that.

The batsmen ran two. And then one of them, over-confident and sure of victory, swung out at a slow, tempting ball from Sitaram, and the ball flew towards Koki in a long, curving arc.

Koki had to run a few yards to her left. Then she leapt like a gazelle and took the ball in both hands. Ranji's team had won, and Koki had made the winning catch.

It was her last appearance as 'twelfth man'. From that day onwards, she was a regular member of the team.

FROM THE POOL TO THE GLACIER

My Boyhood Pool

It was going to rain. I could see the rain moving across the foothills, and I could smell it on the breeze. But instead of turning homewards I pushed my way through the leaves and brambles that grew across the forest path. I had heard the sound of running water at the bottom of the hill, and I was determined to find this hidden stream.

I had to slide down a rock face into a small ravine and there I found the stream running over a bed of shingle, I removed my shoes and started walking upstream. A large, glossy black bird with a curved red beak hooted at me as I passed; and a Paradise Flycatcher—this one I couldn't fail to recognize, with its long fan-tail beating the air—swooped across the stream. Water trickled down from the hillside, from among ferns and grasses and wild flowers; and the hills, rising steeply on either side, kept the ravine in shadow. The rocks were smooth, almost soft, and some of them were grey and some yellow. A small waterfall came down the rocks and formed a deep, round pool of apple-green water.

When I saw the pool, I turned and ran home. I wanted to tell Anil and Kamal about it. It began to rain, but I didn't stop to take shelter, I ran all the way home—through the Sal forest, across the dry river bed through the outskirts of the town.

Though Anil usually chose the adventures we were to have,

the pool was my own discovery, and I was proud of it. 'We'll call it Rusty's Pool,' said Kamal. 'And remember, it's a secret pool. No one else must know of it.'

I think it was the pool that brought us together more than anything else. Kamal was the best swimmer. He dived off rocks and went gliding about under the water like a long golden fish. Anil had strong legs and arms, and he threshed about with much vigour but little skill. I could dive off a rock too, but I usually landed on my stomach.

There were slim silver fish in the stream. At first we tried catching them with a line, but they soon learnt the art of taking the bait without being caught on the hook. Next we tried a bedsheet (Anil had removed it from his mother's laundry), which we stretched across one end of the stream; but the fish wouldn't come anywhere near it. Eventually, Anil, without telling us, procured a stick of gunpowder. And Kamal and I were startled out of an afternoon siesta by a flash across the water and a deafening explosion. Half the hillside tumbled into the pool, and Anil along with it. We got him out, along with a large supply of stunned fish which were too small for eating. Anil, however, didn't want all his work to go to waste; so he roasted the fish over a fire and ate them himself.

The effects of the explosion gave Anil another idea, which was to enlarge our pool by building a dam across one end. This he accomplished with our combined labour. But he had chosen a week when there had been heavy rain in the hills, and we had barely finished the dam when a torrent of water came rushing down the bed of the stream and burst our earthworks, flooding the ravine. Our clothes were carried away by the current, and we had to wait until it was night before creeping into town through the darkest alleyways. Anil was spotted at a street corner, but he posed as a naked sadhu and began calling for alms, and finally slipped in through the back door of his house without being recognized. I had to lend Kamal some of my clothes, and these, being on the small side, made him look odd and gangly. Our other activities at the pool included wrestling and buffalo-riding.

We wrestled on a strip of sand that ran beside the stream. Anil used to often attend wrestling *akharas* and was something of an expert. Kamal and I would usually combine against him, and after five or ten minutes of furious, unscientific struggle, we would usually succeed in flattening Anil into the sand. Kamal would sit on his head, and I would sit on his legs, until he admitted defeat. There was no fun in taking him on singly because he knew too many tricks for us.

We rode on a couple of buffaloes that sometimes came to drink and wallow in the more muddy parts of the stream. Buffaloes are fine, sluggish creatures, always in search of a soft, slushy resting place. We would climb on their backs, and kick and yell and urge them forward; but on no occasion did we succeed in getting them to carry us anywhere. If they tired of our antics, they would merely roll over on their backs, taking us with them into a bed of muddy water.

Not that it mattered how muddy we got because we had only to dive into the pool to get rid of it all. The buffaloes couldn't get to the pool because of its narrow outlet and the slippery rocks.

If it was possible for Anil and me to leave our homes at night, we would come to the pool for a swim by moonlight. We would often find Kamal there before us. He wasn't afraid of the dark or the surrounding forest, where there were panthers and jungle cats. We bathed silently at nights because the stillness of the surrounding jungle seemed to discourage high spirits; but sometimes Kamal would sing—he had a clear, ringing voice—and we would float the red, long-fingered poinsettias downstream.

The pool was to be our principal meeting place during the coming months. It was not that we couldn't meet in town. But the pool was secret, known only to us, and it gave us a feeling of conspiracy and adventure to meet there after school. It was at the pool that we made our plans: it was at the pool that we first spoke of the glacier; but several weeks and a few other exploits were to pass before the particular dream materialized.

Ghosts on the Veranda

Anil's mother's memory was stored with an incredible amount of folklore, and she would sometimes astonish us with her stories of spirits and mischievous ghosts.

One evening, when Anil's father was out of town, and Kamal and I had been invited to stay the night at Anil's upper-storey flat in the bazaar, his mother began to tell us about the various types of ghosts she had known. Mulia, a servant-girl, having just taken a bath, came out on the veranda with her hair loose.

'My girl, you ought not to leave your hair loose like that,' said Anil's mother. 'It is better to tie a knot in it.'

'But I have not oiled it yet,' said Mulia.

'Never mind, but you should not leave your hair loose towards sunset. There are spirits called djinns who are attracted to long hair and pretty black eyes like yours. They may be tempted to carry you away!'

'How dreadful!' exclaimed Mulia, hurriedly tying a knot in her hair and going indoors to be on the safe side. Kamal,

Anil and I sat on a string cot, facing Anil's mother, who sat on another cot. She was not much older than thirty-two, and had often been mistaken for Anil's elder sister; she came from a village near Mathura, a part of the country famous for its gods, spirits and demons.

'Can you see djinns, aunty-ji?' I asked.

'Sometimes,' she said. 'There was an Urdu teacher in Mathura, whose pupils were about the same age as you. One of the boys was very good at his lessons. One day, while he sat at his desk in a corner of the classroom, the teacher asked him to fetch a book from the cupboard which stood at the far end of the room. The boy, who felt lazy that morning, didn't move from his seat. He merely stretched out his hand, took the book from the cupboard, and handed it to the teacher. Everyone was astonished, because the boy's arm had stretched about four yards before touching the book! They realized that he was a djinn; that was the reason for his being so good at games and exercises, which required great agility.'

'Well, I wish I was a djinn,' said Anil. 'Especially for volleyball matches.'

Anil's mother then told us about munjia, a mischievous ghost who lives in lonely Peepul trees. When a munjia is annoyed, he rushes out from his tree and upsets tongas, bullock carts and cycles. Even a bus is known to have been upset by a munjia.

'If you are passing beneath a Peepul tree at night,' warned Anil's mother, 'be careful not to yawn without covering your mouth or snapping your fingers in front of it. If you don't remember to do that, the munjia will jump down your throat and completely ruin your digestion!'

In an attempt to change the subject, Kamal mentioned that a friend of his had found a snake in his bed one morning.

'Did he kill it?' asked Anil's mother anxiously.

'No, it slipped away,' said Kamal.

'Good,' she said. 'It is lucky if you see a snake early in the morning.'

'It won't bite you if you leave it alone,' she said.

By eleven o'clock, after we had finished our dinner and heard a few more ghost stories—including one about Anil's grandmother, whose spirit paid the family a visit—Kamal and I were most reluctant to leave the company on the veranda and retire to the room that had been set apart for us. It did not make us feel any better to be told by Anil's mother that we should recite certain magical verses to keep away the more mischievous spirits. We tried one, which went:

Bhoot, pret, pisach, dana
Chhoo mantar, sab nikal jana,
Mano, mano, Shiv ka kahna...

which, roughly translated, means:

Ghosts, spirits, goblins, sprites,
Away you fly, don't come tonight,
Or with great Shiva you'll have to fight!

Shiva, the Destroyer, is one of the three major Hindu deities.

But the more we repeated the verse, the more uneasy we became, and when I got into bed (after carefully examining it for snakes), I couldn't lie still but kept twisting and turning and looking at the walls for moving shadows. Kamal attempted to raise our spirits by singing softly, but this only made the atmosphere more eerie. After a while we heard someone knocking at the door, and the voices of Anil and the maidservant. Getting up and opening the door, I found them looking pale and anxious.

They, too, had succeeded in frightening themselves as a result of Anil's mother's stories.

'Are you all right?' asked Anil. 'Wouldn't you like to sleep in our part of the house? It might be safer. Mulia will help us carry the beds across!'

'We're quite all right,' protested Kamal and I, refusing to admit we were nervous; but we were hustled along to the other side of the flat as though a band of ghosts was conspiring against us. Anil's mother had been absent during all this activity but suddenly we heard her screaming from the direction of the room we had just left.

'Rusty and Kamal have disappeared!' she cried. 'Their beds have gone, too!'

And then, when she came out on the veranda and saw us dashing about in our pyjamas, she screamed again and collapsed on a cot.

After that, we didn't allow Anil's mother to tell us ghost stories at night.

To the Hills

At the end of August, when the rains were nearly over, we met at the pool to make plans for the autumn holidays. We had bathed and were stretched out in the shade of the fresh, rain-washed Sal trees, when Kamal, pointing vaguely to the distant mountains, said: 'Why don't we go to the Pindari Glacier?'

'The glacier!' exclaimed Anil. 'But that's all snow and ice!'

'Of course it is,' said Kamal. 'But there's a path through the mountains that goes all the way to the foot of the glacier. It's only fifty-four miles!'

'Do you mean we must—*walk* fifty-four miles?'

'Well, there's no other way,' said Kamal. 'Unless you prefer to sit on a mule. But your legs are too long, they'll be trailing along the ground. No, we'll have to walk. It will take us about ten days to get to the glacier and back, but if we take enough food there'll be no problem. There are dak bungalows to stay in at night.'

'Kamal gets all the best ideas,' I said. 'But I suppose Anil and I will have to get our parents' permission. And some money.'

'My mother won't let me go,' said Anil. 'She says the mountains are full of ghosts. And she thinks I'll get up to some mischief. How can one get up to mischief on a lonely mountain?'

'I'm sure it won't be dangerous, people are always going to the glacier. Can you see that peak above the others on the right?' Kamal pointed to the distant snow-range, barely visible against the soft blue sky. 'The Pindari Glacier is below it. It's at 12,000 feet, I think, but we won't need any special equipment. There'll be snow only for the final two or three miles. Do you know that it's the beginning of the river Sarayu?'

'You mean our river?' asked Anil, thinking of the little river that wandered along the outskirts of the town, joining the Ganga further downstream.

'Yes. But it's only a trickle where it starts.'

'How much money will we need?' I asked, determined to be practical.

'Well, I've saved twenty rupees,' said Kamal.

'But won't you need that for your books?' I asked.

'No, this is extra. If each of us brings twenty rupees, we should have enough. There's nothing to spend money on, once we are up on the mountains. There are only one or two villages on the way, and food is scarce, so we'll have to take plenty of food with us. I learnt all this from the Tourist Office.'

'Kamal's been planning this without our knowledge,' complained Anil.

'He always plans in advance,' I said. 'But it's a good idea, and it should be a fine adventure.'

'All right,' said Anil. 'But Rusty will have to be with me when I ask my mother. She thinks Rusty is very sensible and might let me go if he says it's quite safe.' And he ended the discussion by jumping into the pool, where we soon joined him.

Though my mother hesitated about letting me go, my father said it was a wonderful idea, and was only sorry because he couldn't accompany us himself (which was a relief, as we didn't want our parents along); and though Anil's father hesitated—or rather, because he hesitated—his mother said, yes, of course Anil must go, the mountain air would be good for his health. A puzzling remark, because Anil's health had never been better. The bazaar people, when they heard that Anil might be away for a couple of weeks, were overjoyed at the prospect of a quiet spell and pressed his father to let him go.

On a cloudy day promising rain, we bundled ourselves into the bus that was to take us to Kapkote (where people lose their caps and coats, punned Anil), the starting point of our trek. Each of us carried a haversack, and we had also brought along a good-sized bedding roll which, apart from blankets, also contained rice and flour thoughtfully provided by Anil's mother. We had no idea how we would carry the bedding roll once we started walking; but an astrologer had told Anil's mother it was a good day for travelling, so we didn't worry much over minor details.

We were soon in the hills, on a winding road that took us up and up, until we saw the valley and our town spread out beneath us, the river a silver ribbon across the plain. Kamal pointed to a patch of dense Sal forest and said, 'Our pool must be there!' We took a sharp bend, the valley disappeared and the mountains towered above us.

We had dull headaches by the time we reached Kapkote; but when we got down from the bus, a cool breeze freshened us. At the wayside shop, we drank glasses of hot, sweet tea, and the shopkeeper told us we could spend the night in one of his rooms. It was pleasant at Kapkote, the hills wooded with Deodar trees, the lower slopes planted with fresh green paddy. At night there was a wind moaning in the trees, and it found its way through the cracks in the windows and eventually through our blankets. Then, right outside the door, a dog began howling at the moon. It had been a good day for travelling, but the astrologer hadn't warned us that it would be a bad night for sleep.

Next morning, we washed our faces at a small stream about a hundred yards from the shop, and filled our water bottles for the day's march. A boy from the nearby village sat on a rock, studying our movements.

'Where are you going?' he asked, unable to suppress his curiosity.

'To the glacier,' said Kamal.

'Let me come with you,' said the boy. 'I know the way.'

'You're too small,' said Anil. 'We need someone who can carry our bedding roll.'

'I'm small,' said the boy, 'but I'm strong. I'm not a weakling like the boys in the plains.' Though he was shorter than any of us, he certainly looked sturdy and had a muscular, well-knit body and pink cheeks. 'See!' he said, and picking up a rock the size of a football, he heaved it across the stream.

'I think he can come with us,' I said.

And the boy, whose name was Bisnu, dashed off to inform his people of his employment—we had agreed to pay him a rupee a day for acting as our guide and sherpa.

And then we were walking—at first, above the little Sarayu River, then climbing higher along the rough mule track, always within sound of the water. Kamal wanted to bathe in the river. I said it was too far, and Anil said we wouldn't reach the dak bungalow before dark if we went for a swim. Regretfully, we left the river behind and marched on through a forest of oaks, over wet, rotting leaves that made a soft carpet for our feet. We ate at noon, under an oak. As we didn't want to waste any time making a fire—not on this first crucial day—we ate beans from a tin and drank most of our water.

In the afternoon we came to the river again. The water was swifter now, green and bubbling, still far below us. We saw two boys in the water, swimming in an inlet, which reminded us of our own secret pool. They waved and invited us to join them. We returned their greeting; but it would have taken us an hour to get down to the river and up again so we continued on our way.

We walked fifteen miles on the first day—our speed was to decrease after this—and we were at the dak bungalow by six o'clock. Bisnu busied himself collecting sticks for a fire. Anil found the bungalow's watchman asleep in a patch of fading sunlight and roused him. The watchman, who hadn't been bothered by visitors for weeks, grumbled at our intrusion and opened a room for us. He also produced some potatoes from his quarters, and these were roasted for dinner.

It became cold after the sun had gone down, and we remained close to Bisnu's fire. The damp sticks burnt fitfully. But Bisnu had justified his inclusion in our party. He had balanced the bedding roll on his shoulders as though it were full of cotton wool instead of blankets. Now he was helping with the cooking. And we were glad to have him sharing our hot potatoes and strong tea.

There were only two beds in the room. We pushed these together, apportioning out the blankets as fairly as possible. Then the four of us leapt into bed, shivering in the cold. We were already over 5,000 feet. Bisnu, in his own peculiar way, had wrapped a scarf around his neck, though a cotton singlet and shorts were all that he wore for the night.

'Tell us a story, Rusty,' said Anil. 'It will help us fall asleep.'

I told them one of his mother's stories, about a boy and a girl who had been changed into a pair of buffaloes; and then Bisnu told us about the ghost of a sadhu, who was to be seen sitting in the snow by moonlight, not far from the glacier. Far from putting us to sleep, this story kept us awake for hours.

'Aren't you asleep yet?' I asked Anil in the middle of the night.

'No, you keep kicking me,' he lied.

'We don't have enough blankets,' complained Kamal, 'it's too cold to sleep.'

'I never sleep till it's very late,' mumbled Bisnu from the bottom of the bed. No one was prepared to admit that our imaginations were keeping us awake.

After a little while we heard a thud on the corrugated tin sheeting, and then the sound of someone—or something—scrambling about on the roof. Anil, Kamal and I sat up in bed, startled out of our wits. Bisnu, who had been winning the race to be fast asleep, merely turned over on his side and grunted.

'It's only a bear,' he said. 'Didn't you notice the pumpkins on the roof? Bears love pumpkins.'

For half an hour we had to listen to the bear as it clambered about on the roof, feasting on the watchman's ripening pumpkins. Finally, there was silence. Kamal and I crawled out of our blankets and went to the window. And through the frosted glass, we saw a Himalayan black bear ambling across the slope in front of the bungalow, a fat pumpkin held between its paws.

To The River

It was raining when we woke, and the mountains were obscured by a heavy mist. We delayed our departure, playing football on the veranda with one of the pumpkins that had fallen off the roof. At noon, the rain stopped, and the sun shone through the clouds. As the mist lifted, we saw the snow range, the great peaks of Nanda Kot and Trisul stepping into the sky.

'It's different up here,' said Kamal. 'I feel like a different person.'

'That's the altitude,' I said. 'As we go higher, we'll get lighter in the head.'

'Anil is light in the head already,' said Kamal. 'I hope the altitude isn't too much for him.'

'If you two are going to be witty,' said Anil, 'I shall go off with Bisnu, and you'll have to find the way yourselves.'

Bisnu grinned at each of us in turn to show us that he wasn't taking sides; and after a breakfast of boiled eggs, we set off on our trek to the next bungalow.

Rain had made the ground slippery, and we were soon ankle-deep in slush. Our next bungalow lay in a narrow valley, on the banks of the rushing Pindar River, which twisted its way through the mountains. We were not sure how far we had to go, but nobody seemed in a hurry. On an impulse, I decided to hurry ahead of the others. I wanted to be waiting for them at the river.

The path dropped steeply, then rose and went round a big mountain. I met a woodcutter and asked him how far it was to the river. He was a short, stocky man, with gnarled hands and a weathered face.

'Seven miles,' he said. 'Are you alone?'

'No, the others are following, but I cannot wait for them. If you meet them, tell them I'll be waiting at the river.'

The path descended steeply now, and I had to run a little. It was a dizzy, winding path. The hillside was covered with lush green ferns and, in the trees, unseen birds sang loudly. Soon, I was in the valley, and the path straightened out. A girl was coming from the opposite direction. She held a long, curved knife, with which she had been cutting grass and fodder. There were rings in her nose and ears, and her arms were covered with heavy bangles. The bangles made music when she moved her hands—it was as though her hands spoke a language of their own.

'How far is it to the river?' I asked.

The girl had probably never been near the river, or she may have been thinking of another one, because she replied, 'Twenty miles,' without any hesitation.

I laughed, and ran down the path. A parrot screeched suddenly, flew low over my head—a flash of blue and green—and took the course of the path while I followed its dipping flight until the path rose and the bird disappeared into the trees.

A trickle of water came from the hillside, and I stopped to drink. The water was cold and sharp and very refreshing. I had walked alone for nearly an hour. Presently I saw a boy ahead of me, driving a few goats along the path.

'How far is it to the river?' I asked, when I caught up with him.

The boy said, 'Oh, not far, just around the next hill.'

As I was hungry, I produced some dry bread from my pocket and, breaking it in two, offered half to the boy. We sat on the grassy hillside and ate in silence. Then we walked on together and began talking; and I did not notice the smarting of my feet and the distance I had covered. But after some time, the boy had to diverge along another path, and I was once more on my own.

I missed the village boy. I looked up and down the path, but I could see no one, no sign of Anil, Kamal and Bisnu, and the river was not in sight either. I began to feel discouraged. But I couldn't turn back; I was determined to be at the river before the others.

And so I walked on, along the muddy path, past terraced fields and small stone houses, until there were no more fields and houses, only forest and sun and silence.

The silence was oppressive and a little frightening. It was different from the silence of a room or an empty street. Neither was there any movement, except for the bending of grass beneath my feet, and the circling of a hawk high above the Fir trees.

And then, as I rounded a sharp bend, the silence broke into sound.

The sound of the river.

Far down in the valley, the river tumbled over itself in its impatience to reach the plains. I began to run, slipped and stumbled, but continued running. The water was blue and white and wonderful.

When Anil, Kamal and Bisnu arrived, the four of us bravely decided to bathe in the little river. The late afternoon sun was still warm, but the water—so clear and inviting—proved to be ice-cold. Only twenty miles upstream, the river emerged as a little trickle from the glacier, and in its swift descent down the mountain slopes, it did not give the sun a chance to penetrate its waters. But we were determined to bathe, to wash away the dust and sweat of our two days' trudging, and we leapt about in the shallows like startled porpoises, slapping water on each other and gasping with the shock of each immersion. Bisnu, more accustomed to mountain streams than us, ventured across in an attempt to catch an otter, but wasn't fast enough. Then we were on the springy grass, wrestling each other in order to get warm.

The bungalow stood on a ledge just above the river, and the sound of the water rushing down the mountain defile could be heard at all times. The sound of the birds, which we had grown used to, was drowned by the sound of the water; but the birds could be seen, many-coloured, standing out splendidly against the dark green forest foliage: the red-crowned jay, the paradise flycatcher, the purple whistling-thrush, others we could not recognize.

Higher up the mountain, above some terraced land where oats and barley were grown, stood a small cluster of huts. This, we were told by the watchman, was the last village on the way to the glacier. It was, in fact, one of the last villages in India because if we crossed the difficult passes beyond the glacier, we would find ourselves in Tibet. We told the watchman we would be quite satisfied if we reached the glacier.

Then Anil made the mistake of mentioning the Abominable Snowman, of whom we had been reading in the papers. The people of Nepal believe in the existence of the Snowman, and our watchman was a Nepali.

'Yes, I have seen the Yeti,' he told us. 'A great shaggy flat-footed creature. In the winter, when it snows heavily, he passes by the bungalow at night. I have seen his tracks the next morning.'

'Does he come this way in the summer?' I asked anxiously. We were sitting before another of Bisnu's fires, drinking tea with condensed milk, and trying to get through a black, sticky sweet, which the watchman had produced from his tin trunk.

'The Yeti doesn't come here in the summer,' said the old man. 'But I have seen the Lidini sometimes. You have to be careful of her.'

'What is a Lidini?' asked Kamal.

'Ah!' said the watchman mysteriously. 'You have heard of the Abominable Snowman, no doubt, but there are few who have heard of the Abominable Snowwoman! And yet she is by far the more dangerous of the two!'

'What is she like?' asked Anil, and we all craned forward.

'She is of the same height as the Yeti—about seven feet when her back is straight—and her hair is much longer. She has very long teeth and nails. Her feet face inwards, but she can run very fast, especially downhill. If you see a Lidini, and she chases you, always run away in an uphill direction. She tires quickly because of her feet. But when running downhill she has no trouble at all, and you have to be very fast to escape her!'

'Well, we're all good runners,' said Anil with a nervous laugh, 'but it's just a fairy story, I don't believe a word of it.'

'But you *must* believe fairy stories,' I said, remembering a performance of Peter Pan in London, when those in the audience who believed in fairies were asked to clap their hands in order to save Tinker Bell's life. 'Even if they aren't true,' I added, deciding there was a world of difference between Tinker Bell and the Abominable Snowwoman.

'Well, I don't believe there's a Snowman or a Snow woman!' declared Anil.

The watchman was most offended and refused to tell us anything about the Sagpa and Sagpani; but Bisnu knew about them, and later, when we were in bed, he told us that they were similar to Snowmen but much smaller. Their favourite pastime was sleeping, and they became very annoyed if anyone woke them, became ferocious and did not give one much time to start running uphill. The Sagpa and Sagpani sometimes kidnapped small children, and taking them to their cave, they would look after the children very carefully, feeding them fruits, honey, rice and earthworms.

'When the Sagpa isn't looking,' he said, 'you can throw the earthworms over your shoulder.'

The Glacier

It was a fine sunny morning when we set out to cover the last seven miles to the glacier. We had expected this to be a stiff climb, but the last dak bungalow was situated at well over 10,000 feet above sea level, and the ascent was fairly gradual.

And suddenly, there were no more trees. As the bungalow dropped out of sight, the trees and bushes gave way to short grass and little blue and pink alpine flowers. The snow peaks were close now, ringing us in on every side. We passed waterfalls, cascading hundreds of feet down precipitous rock faces, thundering into the little river. A great golden eagle hovered over us for some time.

'I feel different again,' said Kamal.

'We're very high now,' I said. 'I hope we won't get headaches.'

'I've got one already,' complained Anil. 'Let's have some tea.'

We had left our cooking utensils at the bungalow, expecting

to return there for the night and had brought with us only a few biscuits, chocolate and a thermos of tea. We finished the tea, and Bisnu scrambled about on the grassy slopes, collecting wild strawberries. They were tiny strawberries, very sweet, and they did nothing to satisfy our appetites. There was no sign of habitation or human life.

The only creatures to be found at that height were the gorals—sure-footed mountain goats—and an occasional snow leopard or a bear.

We found and explored a small cave, and then, turning a bend, came unexpectedly upon the glacier. The hill fell away, and there, confronting us, was a great white field of snow and ice, cradled between two peaks that could only have been the abode of the gods. We were speechless for several minutes. Kamal took my hand and held on to it for reassurance; perhaps he was not sure that what he saw was real. Anil's mouth hung open. Bisnu's eyes glittered with excitement.

We proceeded cautiously on the snow, supporting each other on the slippery surface; but we could not go far, because we were quite unequipped for any high-altitude climbing. It was pleasant to feel that we were the only boys in our town who had climbed so high. A few black rocks jutted out from the snow, and we sat down on them, to feast our eyes on the view. The sun reflected sharply from the snow, and we felt surprisingly warm.

'Let's sunbathe!' said Anil, on a sudden impulse.

'Yes, let's do that!' I said.

In a few minutes we had taken off our clothes and, sitting on the rocks, were exposing ourselves to the elements. It was delicious to feel the sun crawling over my skin. Within half an hour I was postbox red, and so was Bisnu, and the two of us decided to get into our clothes before the sun scorched the skin off our backs. Kamal and Anil appeared to be more resilient to sunlight and laughed at our discomfiture. Bisnu and I avenged ourselves by gathering up handfuls of snow and rubbing it on their backs. We dressed quickly enough after that, Anil leaping about like a performing monkey.

Meanwhile, almost imperceptibly, clouds had covered some of the peaks, and white mist drifted down the mountain slopes. It was time to get back to the bungalow; we would barely make it before dark. We had not gone far when lightning began to sizzle about the mountaintops followed by waves of thunder.

'Let's run!' shouted Anil. 'We can shelter in the cave!'

The clouds could hold themselves in no longer, and the rain came down suddenly, stinging our faces as it was whipped up by an icy wind. Half-blinded, we ran as fast as we could along the slippery path, and stumbled, drenched and exhausted, into the little cave. It was mercifully dry, and not very dark. We remained at the entrance, watching the rain sweep past us, listening to the wind whistling down the long gorge.

'It will take some time to stop,' said Kamal.

'No, it will pass soon,' said Bisnu. 'These storms are short and fierce.'

Anil produced his pocketknife, and to pass the time, we carved our names in the smooth rock of the cave.

'We will come here again, when we are older,' said Kamal, 'and perhaps our names will still be here.'

It had grown dark by the time the rain stopped. A full moon helped us find our way, we went slowly and carefully. The rain had loosened the earth, and stones kept rolling down the hillside. I was afraid of starting a landslide.

'I hope we don't meet the Lidini now,' said Anil fervently.

'I thought you didn't believe in her,' I said.

'I don't,' replied Anil. 'But what if I'm wrong?'

We saw only a mountain goat, the goral, poised on the brow of a precipice, silhouetted against the sky.

And then the path vanished.

Had it not been for the bright moonlight, we might have walked straight into an empty void. The rain had caused a landslide, and where there had been a narrow path, there was now only a precipice of loose, slippery shale.

'We'll have to go back,' said Bisnu. 'It will be too dangerous to try and cross in the dark.'

'We'll sleep in the cave,' I suggested.

'We've nothing to sleep in,' said Anil. 'Not a single blanket between us and nothing to eat!'

'We'll just have to rough it till morning,' said Kamal. 'It will be better than breaking our necks here.'

We returned to the cave, which did at least have the virtue of being dry. Bisnu had matches, and he made a fire with some dry sticks, which had been left in the cave by a previous party. We ate what was left of a loaf of bread.

There was no sleep for any of us that night. We lay close to each other for comfort, but the ground was hard and uneven. And every noise we heard outside the cave made us think of leopards, bears and even the Abominable Snowmen.

We got up as soon as there was a faint glow in the sky. The snow peaks were bright pink, but we were too tired, hungry and worried to care for the beauty of the sunrise. We took the path to the landslide, and once again, looked for a way across. Kamal ventured to take a few steps on the loose pebbles, but the ground gave way immediately, and we had to grab him by the arms and shoulders to prevent him from sliding a hundred feet down the gorge.

'Now what are we going to do?' I asked.

'Look for another way,' said Bisnu.

'But do you know of any?'

We all turned to look at Bisnu, expecting him to provide the solution to our problem.

'I have heard of a way,' said Bisnu, 'but I have never used it. It will be a little dangerous, I think. The path has not been used for several years—not since the traders stopped coming in from Tibet.'

'Never mind, we'll try it,' said Anil.

'We will have to cross the glacier first,' said Bisnu. 'That's the main problem.'

We looked at each other in silence. The glacier didn't look difficult to cross, but we knew that it would not be easy for novices. For almost two furlongs, it consisted of hard, slippery ice.

Anil was the first to arrive at a decision.

'Come on,' he said. 'There's no time to waste.'

We were soon on the glacier. And we remained on it for a long time. For every two steps forward, we slid one step backward. Our progress was slow and awkward. Sometimes, after advancing several yards across the ice at a steep incline, one of us would slip back and the others would have to slither down to help him up. At one particularly difficult spot, I dropped our water bottle and, grabbing at it, lost my footing, fell and went sliding some twenty feet down the ice slope.

I sprained my wrist and hurt my knee and was to prove a liability for the rest of the trek.

Kamal tied his handkerchief around my hand, and Anil took charge of the water bottle, which we had filled with ice. Using my good hand to grab Bisnu's legs whenever I slipped, I struggled on behind the others.

It was almost noon and we were quite famished when we put our feet on grass again. And then we had another steep climb, clutching at roots and grasses, before we reached the path that Bisnu had spoken about. It was little more than a goat track, but it took us around the mountain and brought us within sight of the dak bungalow.

'I could eat a whole chicken,' said Kamal.

'I could eat two,' I said.

'I could eat a Snowman,' said Bisnu.

'And I could eat the chowkidar,' said Anil.

Fortunately for the chowkidar, he had anticipated our hunger; and when we staggered into the bungalow late in the afternoon, we found a meal waiting for us. True, there was no chicken—but, so ravenous did we feel, that even the lowly onion tasted delicious!

We had Bisnu to thank for getting us back successfully. He had brought us over mountain and glacier with all the skill and confidence of a boy who had the Himalaya in his blood.

We took our time getting back to Kapkote; fished in the Sarayu River; bathed with the village boys we had seen on our way up; collected strawberries, ferns and wild flowers; and finally said goodbye to Bisnu.

Anil wanted to take Bisnu along with us, but the boy's parents refused to let him go, saying that he was too young for the life of a city; but we were of the opinion that Bisnu could have taught the city boys a few things.

'Never mind,' said Kamal. 'We'll go on another trip next year, and we'll take you with us, Bisnu. We'll write and let you know our plans.'

This promise made Bisnu happy, and he saw us off at the bus stop, shouldering our bedding to the end. Then he skimmed up the trunk of a fir tree to have a better view of us leaving, and we saw him waving to us from the tree as our bus went round the bend from Kapkote, the hills were left behind and the plains stretched out below.

ADVENTURES IN READING

1

You don't see them so often now, those tiny books and almanacs—genuine pocket books—once so popular with our parents and grandparents; much smaller than the average paperback, often smaller than the palm of the hand. With the advent of coffee-table books, new books keep growing bigger and bigger, rivalling tombstones! And one day, like Alice after drinking from the wrong bottle, they will reach the ceiling and won't have anywhere else to go. The average publisher, who apparently believes that large profits are linked to large books, must look upon these old miniatures with amusement or scorn. They were not meant for a coffee table, true. They were meant for true book lovers and readers, for they took up very little space—you could slip them into your pocket without any discomfort, either to you or the pocket.

I have a small collection of these little books, treasured over the years. Foremost is my father's prayer book and psalter, with his name, 'Aubrey Bond, Lovedale, 1917', inscribed on the inside back cover. Lovedale is a school in the Nilgiri Hills in South India, where, as a young man, he did his teacher's training. He gave it to me soon after I went to a boarding school in Shimla in 1944, and my own name is inscribed on it in his beautiful handwriting.

Another beautiful little prayer book in my collection is called

The Finger Prayer Book. Bound in soft leather, it is about the same length and breadth as the average middle finger. Replete with psalms, it is the complete book of common prayer and not an abridgement; a marvel of miniature book production.

Not much larger is a delicate item in calf leather, *The Humour of Charles Lamb*. It fits into my wallet and often stays there. It has a tiny portrait of the great essayist, followed by some thirty to forty extracts from his essays, such as this favourite of mine: 'Every dead man must take upon himself to be lecturing me with his odious truism, that "Such as he is now, I must shortly be". Not so shortly friend, perhaps as thou imaginest. In the meantime, I am alive. I move about. I am worth twenty of thee. Know thy betters!'

No fatalist, Lamb. He made no compromise with Father Time. He affirmed that in age we must be as glowing and tempestuous as in youth! And yet Lamb is thought to be an old-fashioned writer.

Another favourite among my 'little' books is *The Pocket Trivet, An Anthology for Optimists*, published by *The Morning Post* newspaper in 1932. 'But what is a trivet?', the unenlightened may well ask. Well, it's a stand for a small pot or kettle, fixed securely over a grate. To be right as a trivet is to be perfectly right. Just right, like the short sayings in this book, which is further enlivened by a number of charming woodcuts based on the seventeenth century originals; such as the illustration of a moth hovering over a candle flame and below it the legend—'I seeke mine owne hurt.'

But the sayings are mostly of a cheering nature, such as Emerson's 'Hitch your wagon to a star!' or the West Indian proverb: 'Every day no Christmas, an' every day no rainy day.'

My book of trivets is a happy example of much concentrated

wisdom being collected in a small space—the beauty separated from the dross. It helps me to forget the dilapidated building in which I live and to look instead at the ever-changing cloud patterns as seen from my bedroom windows. There is no end to the shapes made by the clouds, or to the stories they set off in my head. We don't have to circle the world in order to find beauty and fulfilment. After all, most of living has to happen in the mind. And, to quote one anonymous sage from my trivet, 'The world is only the size of each man's head.'

2

Among the current fraternity of writers, I must be that very rare person—an author who actually writes by hand!

Soon after the invention of the typewriter, most editors and publishers understandably refused to look at any mansucript that was handwritten. A decade or two earlier, when Dickens and Balzac had submitted their hefty manuscrips in longhand, no one had raised any objection. Had their handwriting been awful, their manuscripts would still have been read. Fortunately for all concerned, most writers, famous or obscure, took pains over their handwriting. For some, it was an art in itself, and many of those early manuscripts are a pleasure to look at and read.

And it wasn't only authors who wrote with an elegant hand. Parents and grandparents of most of us had distinctive styles of their own. I still have my father's last letter, written to me when I was at boarding school in Shimla some fifty years ago. He used large, beautifully formed letters, and his thoughts seemed to have the same flow and clarity as his handwriting.

In his letter he advises me (then a nine-year-old) about my own handwriting: 'I wanted to write before about your writing. Ruskin... Sometimes I get letters from you in very small writing, as if you wanted to squeeze everything into one sheet of letter paper. It is not good for you or for your eyes, to get into the habit of writing too small... Try and form a larger style of handwriting—use more paper if necessary!'

I did my best to follow his advice, and I'm glad to report that after nearly forty years of the writing life, most people can still read my handwriting!

Word processors are all the rage now, and I have no objection to these mechanical aids any more than I have to my old Olympia typewriter, made in 1956 and still going strong. Although I do all my writing in longhand, I follow the conventions by typing a second draft. But I would not enjoy my writing if I had to do it straight on to a machine. It isn't just the pleasure of writing longhand. I like taking my notebooks and writing pads to odd places. This particular essay is being written on the steps of my small cottage facing Pari Tibba (Fairy Hill). Part of the reason for sitting here is that there is a new postman on this route, and I don't want him to miss me.

For a freelance writer, the postman is almost as important as a publisher. I could, of course, sit here doing nothing, but as I have pencil and paper with me, and feel like using them, I shall write until the postman comes and maybe after he has gone, too! There is really no way in which I could set up a word processor on these steps.

There are a number of favourite places where I do my writing. One is under the chestnut tree on the slope above the cottage. Word processors were not designed keeping mountain slopes in mind. But armed with a pen (or pencil) and paper, I can lie on the grass and write for hours. On one occasion, last month, I did take my typewriter into the garden, and I am still trying to extricate an acorn from under the keys, while the roller seems permanently stained yellow with some fine pollen dust from the Deodar trees.

My friends keep telling me about all the wonderful things I can do with a word processor, but they haven't got around to finding me one that I can take to bed, for that is another place where I do much of my writing—especially on cold winter nights, when it is impossible to keep the cottage warm.

While the wind howls outside, and snow piles up on the windowsill, I am warm under my quilt, writing pad on my knees, ballpoint pen at the ready. And if, next day, the weather is warm and sunny, these simple aids will accompany me on a long walk, ready for instant use should I wish to record an incident, a prospect, a conversation or simply a train of thought.

When I think of the great eighteenth- and nineteenth-century writers, scratching away with their quill pens, filling hundreds of pages every month, I am amazed to find that their handwriting did not deteriorate into the sort of hieroglyphics that often make up the average doctor's prescription today. They knew they had to write legibly, if only for the sake of the typesetters.

Both Dickens and Thackeray had good, clear, flourishing styles. (Thackeray was a clever illustrator, too). Somerset Maugham had an upright, legible hand. Churchill's neat handwriting never wavered, even when he was under stress. I like the bold, clear, straighforward hand of Abraham Lincoln; it mirrors the man. Mahatma Gandhi, another great soul who fell to the assassin's bullet, had many similarities of both handwriting and outlook.

Not everyone had a beautiful hand. King Henry VIII had an untidy scrawl, but then, he was not a man of much refinement. Guy Fawkes, who tried to blow up the British Parliament, had a very shaky hand. With such a quiver, no wonder he failed in his attempt! Hitler's signature is ugly, as you would expect.

And Napoleon's doesn't seem to know where to stop; how much like the man!

I think my father was right when he said handwriting was often the key to a man's character, and that large, well-formed letters went with an uncluttered mind. Florence Nightingale had a lovely handwriting, the hand of a caring person. And there were many like her among our forebears.

3

When I was a small boy, no Christmas was really complete unless my Christmas stocking contained several recent issues of my favourite comic paper. If today my friends complain that I am too voracious a reader of books, they have only these comics to blame; for they were the origin, if not of my tastes in reading then certainly of the reading habit itself.

I like to think that my conversion to comics began at the age of five, with a comic strip on the children's page of *The Statesman.* In the late 1930s, Benji, whose head later appeared only on the Benji League badge, had a strip to himself; I don't remember his adventures very clearly, but every day (or was it once a week?) I would cut out the Benji strip and paste it into a scrapbook. Two years later, this scrapbook, bursting with the adventures of Benji, accompanied me to boarding school, where, of course, it passed through several hands before finally passing into limbo.

Of course, comics did not form the only reading matter that found its way into my Christmas stocking. Before I was eight, I had read *Peter Pan, Alice,* and most of *Mr Midshipman Easy*; but I had also consumed thousands of comic papers which were, after all, slim affairs and mostly pictorial, 'certain little penny books radiant with gold and rich with bad pictures', as Leigh Hunt described the children's papers of his own time.

But though they were mostly pictorial, comics in those days did have a fair amount of reading matter, too. *The Hostspur, Wizard, Magnet* (a victim of the Second World War) and *Champion* contained stories woven round certain popular characters. In *Champion*, which I read regularly right through my prep school years, there was Rockfist Rogan, RAF, a pugilist who managed to combine boxing with bombing, and Fireworks Flynn, a footballer who always scored the winning goal in the last two minutes of play.

Billy Bunter has, of course, become one of the immortals—almost a subject for literary and social historians. Quite recently, *The Times Literary Supplement* devoted its first two pages to an analysis of the Bunter stories. Eminent lawyers and doctors still look back nostalgically to the arrival of the weekly *Magnet*; they are now the principal customers for the special souvenir edition of the first issue of the *Magnet*, recently reprinted in facsimile. Bunter, 'forever young', has become a folk hero. He is seen on stage, screen and television, and is even quoted in the House of Commons.

From this, I take courage. My only regret is that I did not preserve my own early comics—not because of any bibliophilic value, which they might possess today, but because of my sentimental regard for early influences in art and literature.

The first venture in children's publishing, in 1774, was a comic of sorts. In that year, John Newberry brought out:

> According to Act of Parliament (neatly bound and gilt): A Little Pretty Pocket-Book, intended for the Instruction and Amusement of Little Master Tommy and Pretty Miss Polly, with an agreeable Letter to read from Jack the Giant-Killer...

The book contained pictures, rhymes and games. Newberry's characters and imaginary authors included Woglog the Giant, Tommy Trip, Giles Gingerbread, Nurse Truelove, Peregrine Puzzlebrains, Primrose Prettyface and many others with names similar to those found in the comic papers of our own century.

Newberry was also the originator of the 'Amazing Free Offer', so much a part of American comics. At the beginning of 1755, he had this to offer:

> Nurse Truelove's New Year Gift, or the Book of Books for children, adorned with Cuts and designed as a Present for every little boy who would become a great Man and ride upon a fine Horse; and to every little Girl who would become a great Woman and ride in a Lord Mayor's gilt Coach. Printed for the Author, who has ordered these books to be given gratis to all little Boys in St. Paul's churchyard, they paying for the Binding, which is only Two pence each Book.

Many of today's comics are crude and, like many television serials, violent in their appeal. But I did not know American comics until I was twelve, and by then I had become quite discriminating. Superman, Bulletman, Batman and Green Lantern, and other super heroes all left me cold. I had, by then, passed into the world of real books but the weakness for the comic strip remains. I no longer receive comics in my Christmas stocking, but I do place a few in the stockings of Gautam and Siddharth. And, needless to say, I read them right through beforehand.

THE VISITOR

Amir was sitting on his bed, staring out of the door that opened out onto the roof. A bald mynah bird stared back at him. Then he heard someone calling from downstairs.

'Does anyone live up there?'

'No,' shouted Amir. 'Nobody lives up here.'

'Then can I come up?' asked the person below.

Amir didn't answer. Presently he heard footsteps coming up. The mynah bird flew off the roof and settled in a mango tree.

A boy stood in the doorway, smiling at Amir. He was a little taller than Amir and much thinner. He wore a white shirt outside striped pyjamas. On his feet were open slippers. A tray hung from his shoulders, filled with an assortment of goods.

'Would you like to buy something?' he asked.

In his tray were combs, buttons, reels of thread, shoelaces and little vials of cheap perfume.

'I have everything you need,' he said.

'I don't need anything,' said Amir.

'You need buttons.'

'I don't.'

'Your top button is missing.'

Amir felt for the top button of his shirt and was surprised to find it missing.

'I don't like buttoning my shirt,' he said.

'That's different,' said his visitor and looked him up and down for further signs of wear and tear. 'You'd better buy a new pair of shoelaces.'

Amir looked down at his shoes and said, 'I've got laces.'

'Very poor quality,' said the boy, and taking hold of one of the laces, he tugged at it and snapped it in two.

'See how easily it breaks? Now you need laces.'

'Well, I'm not buying any,' said Amir.

The boy sighed, shrugged, and moved towards the door. As he walked slowly down the steps, Amir stood in the doorway, watching him go. On an impulse, he called out, 'What's your name?'

'Mohan,' replied the boy.

'Well, come again in a week,' said Amir. 'I may need something then.'

◆

Amir went downstairs for his lunch. He returned to his room to study, but dozed off instead. Towards the evening, he felt hungry and restless. He could not remain in his room when everyone else was pouring onto the streets to shop, talk, eat and visit the cinema.

From the roof, he could see the bazaar lights coming on, and hear the jingle of tonga bells and the blare of bus horns. It was a cool evening and he put on his coat before going downstairs.

It was not easy to walk fast on the road to the bazaar. Apart from the great number of pedestrians, there were cyclists and scooter-rickshaws, handcarts and cows, all making movement difficult. A little tea shop was playing film music over a loudspeaker, adding noise to the general confusion.

The balloon man was having a trying time. He was surrounded by a swarm of children who were more intent on bursting his balloons than on buying any. One or two got loose and went sailing over the heads of the crowd to burst over the fire in the chaat shop.

Amir stood outside the chaat shop and ate a variety of spicy snacks. Then he wiped his fingers on the banana leaves on which he had been served and moved on down the bazaar road.

Towards the clock tower, the road grew wider and less crowded. There was a street lamp at the corner of the road. A boy was sitting on the pavement beneath the lamp, bent over a book, absorbed in what he was reading. He seemed not to notice the noise of the bazaar or the chill in the air. As Amir came nearer, he saw that the boy was Mohan.

He did not know whether to stop and talk to him, or carry on down the road. After walking some distance, he felt ashamed at not having stopped to greet the boy, so he turned and retraced his steps. But when he came to the lamp post, Mohan had gone.

When Mohan came again he did not call out from below but came straight up to the room. He looked at Amir's shirt and shoes and saw that one of the shoes was still done up with half a lace. With an air of triumph he dropped a pair of shoelaces on the desk.

'I can't pay for them now,' said Amir.

'You can pay me later.'

Amir sat on the edge of his table while Mohan leant against the wall.

'Do you go to school?' asked Amir.

'Sometimes I go to evening classes,' Mohan said. 'I am sitting privately for my high school exams next month. If I pass...'

He stopped to think about the things he could do if he passed. The way to a career would be open to him, he could study further, become an engineer, or a scientist or an administrator. No more selling combs and buttons at street corners...

'Where are your parents?' asked Amir.

'My father is dead. My mother is in our village in the hills. I have brothers and sisters at home, but I am the only one old enough to work.'

'Then where do you stay?'

'Anywhere. On somebody's veranda or on the maidan; it doesn't matter much in the summer. These days I sleep on the station platform. It's quite warm there.'

'You can sleep here,' said Amir.

◆

One morning, when he opened the door of his room, Amir found Mohan asleep at the top of the steps. He had wrapped himself up in a thin blanket. His tray of merchandise lay a short distance away.

Amir shook him gently and he woke up immediately, blinking in the bright sunlight.

'Why didn't you come in?' asked Amir. 'Why didn't you let me know you were here?'

'It was late,' said Mohan. 'I did not want to wake you. Besides, it was a fine night, not too cold.'

'Someone could have stolen your things. '

Amir made Mohan promise to sleep in the room that night. He came quite early. Amir lent him another blanket, and he lay down on the floor mat and slept soundly while Amir stayed awake worrying if his guest was comfortable enough.

Mohan came quite often, leaving early in the morning before Amir could offer him a meal. He ate at little places in the bazaar.

The high school exams were nearing, and Mohan sat up late with his books. Apart from his occasional evening classes, he received no teaching.

The exams lasted for ten days, and during this time Mohan put aside his tray of odds and ends. He did his papers with confidence. He thought he had done rather well. And when it was over, he took up his tray again and walked all over the town, trying to make up for lost sales.

◆

On the day the exam results were due, Amir rose early. He got to the news agency at five o'clock, just as the morning papers arrived. Bhartu gave him a paper to look at, and he found the page on which the results were listed. He looked down the 'passes' column for the town, but couldn't find Mohan's number on the list. He looked twice to make sure, and then returned the paper to Bhartu with a glum look.

'Failed?' said Bhartu.

Amir nodded and turned away. When he returned to the room, he found Mohan sitting at the top of the steps. He didn't have to tell him anything. Mohan knew by the look on the other's face.

Amir sat down beside him, and they said nothing for a while.

'Never mind,' said Mohan. 'I'll pass next year.' It seemed that Amir was more in need of comforting than himself.

'If only you'd had more time,' said Amir.

'I have plenty of time now. Another year… Can I still stay in your room?'

'For as long as it's my room. That means I shall have to work too, otherwise my grandfather will drag me downstairs again.'

Mohan laughed and went into the room. When he came out, the tray was hanging from his shoulders.

'What would you like to buy?' he asked. 'I have everything you need.'

THE TROUBLE WITH DJINNS

My friend Jimmy has only one arm. He lost the other when he was a young man of twenty-five. The story of how he lost his good right arm is a little difficult to believe, but I swear that it is absolutely true.

To begin with, Jimmy was (and presumably still is) a djinn. Now a djinn isn't really a human like us. A djinn is a spirit creature from another world who has assumed, for a lifetime, the physical aspect of a human being. Jimmy was a true djinn and he had the djinn's gift of being able to elongate his arm at will. Most djinns can stretch their arms to a distance of twenty or thirty feet. Jimmy could attain forty feet. His arm would move through space or up walls or along the ground like a beautiful gliding serpent. I have seen him stretched out beneath a mango tree, helping himself to ripe mangoes from the top of the tree. He loved mangoes. He was a natural glutton and it was probably his gluttony that first led him to misuse his peculiar gifts.

We were at school together at a hill station in northern India. Jimmy was particularly good at basketball. He was clever enough not to lengthen his arm too much because he did not want anyone to know that he was a djinn. In the boxing ring, he generally won his fights. His opponents never seemed to get past his amazing reach. He just kept tapping them on the nose until they retired from the ring, bloody and bewildered.

It was during the half-term examinations that I stumbled on Jimmy's secret. We had been set a particularly difficult algebra paper, but I had managed to cover a couple of sheets with correct answers and was about to forge ahead on another sheet when I noticed someone's hand on my desk. At first I thought it was the invigilator's. But when I looked up there was no one beside me.

Could it be the boy sitting directly behind? No, he was engrossed in his question paper and had his hands to himself. Meanwhile, the hand on my desk had grasped my answer sheets and was cautiously moving off. Following its descent, I found that it was attached to an arm of amazing length and pliability. This moved stealthily down the desk and slithered across the floor, shrinking all the while, until it was restored to its normal length. Its owner was of course one who had never been any good at algebra.

I had to write out my answers a second time but after the exam, I went straight up to Jimmy, told him I didn't like his game and threatened to expose him. He begged me not to let anyone know, assured me that he couldn't really help himself and offered to be of service to me whenever I wished. It was tempting to have Jimmy as my friend, for with his long reach he would obviously be useful. I agreed to overlook the matter of the pilfered papers and we became the best of pals.

It did not take me long to discover that Jimmy's gift was more of a nuisance than a constructive aid. That was because Jimmy had a second-rate mind and did not know how to make proper use of his powers. He seldom rose above the trivial. He used his long arm in the tuck shop, in the classroom, in the dormitory. And when we were allowed out to the cinema, he used it in the dark of the hall.

Now the trouble with all djinns is that they have a weakness for women with long black hair. The longer and blacker the hair, the better for djinns. And should a djinn manage to take possession of the woman he desires, she goes into a decline and her beauty decays. Everything about her is destroyed except for the beautiful long black hair.

Jimmy was still too young to be able to take possession in this way, but he couldn't resist touching and stroking long black hair. The cinema was the best place for the indulgence of his whims. His arm would start stretching, his fingers would feel their way along the rows of seats, and his lengthening limb would slowly work its way along the aisle until it reached the back of the seat in which sat the object of his admiration. His hand would stroke the long black hair with great tenderness and if the girl felt anything and looked round, Jimmy's hand would disappear behind the seat and lie there poised like the hood of a snake, ready to strike again.

At college two or three years later, Jimmy's first real victim succumbed to his attentions. She was a lecturer in economics, not very good looking, but her hair, black and lustrous, reached almost to her knees. She usually kept it in plaits but Jimmy saw her one morning just after she had taken a head bath, and her hair lay spread out on the cot on which she was reclining. Jimmy could no longer control himself. His spirit, the very essence of his personality, entered the woman's body and the next day she was distraught, feverish and excited. She would not eat, went into a coma and in a few days dwindled to a mere skeleton. When she died, she was nothing but skin and bone but her hair had lost none of its loveliness.

I took pains to avoid Jimmy after this tragic event. I could not prove that he was the cause of the lady's sad demise but in my own heart, I was quite certain of it. For since meeting Jimmy, I had read a good deal about djinns and knew their ways.

We did not see each other for a few years. And then, holidaying in the hills last year, I found we were staying at the same hotel. I could not very well ignore him and after we had drunk a few beers together I began to feel that I had perhaps misjudged Jimmy and that he was not the irresponsible djinn I had taken him for. Perhaps the college lecturer had died of some mysterious malady that attacks only college lecturers and Jimmy had nothing at all to do with it.

We had decided to take our lunch and a few bottles of beer to a grassy knoll just below the main motor road. It was late afternoon and I had been sleeping off the effects of the beer when I woke to find Jimmy looking rather agitated.

'What's wrong?' I asked.

'Up there, under the pine trees,' he said. 'Just above the road. Don't you see them?'

'I see two girls,' I said. 'So what?'

'The one on the left. Haven't you noticed her hair?'

'Yes, it is very long and beautiful and—now look, Jimmy, you'd better get a grip on yourself!' But already his hand was out of sight, his arm snaking up the hillside and across the road.

Presently I saw the hand emerge from some bushes near the girls and then cautiously make its way to the girl with the black tresses. So absorbed was Jimmy in the pursuit of his favourite pastime that he failed to hear the blowing of a horn. Around the bend of the road came a speeding Mercedes Benz truck.

Jimmy saw the truck but there wasn't time for him to shrink his arm back to normal. It lay right across the entire width of the road and when the truck had passed over it, it writhed and twisted like a mortally wounded python.

By the time the truck driver and I could fetch a doctor, the arm (or what was left of it) had shrunk to its ordinary size. We took Jimmy to hospital where the doctors found it necessary to amputate. The truck driver, who kept insisting that the arm he ran over was at least thirty feet long, was arrested on a charge of drunken driving.

Some weeks later I asked Jimmy, 'Why are you so depressed? You still have one arm. Isn't it gifted in the same way?'

'I never tried to find out,' he said, 'and I'm not going to try now.'

He is, of course, still a djinn at heart and whenever he sees a girl with long black hair he must be terribly tempted to try out his one good arm and stroke her beautiful tresses. But he has learnt his lesson. It is better to be a human without any gifts than a djinn or a genius with one too many.

OUR GREAT ESCAPE

It had been a lonely winter for a fourteen-year-old. I had spent the first few weeks of the vacation with my mother and stepfather in Dehra. Then they left for Delhi, and I was pretty much on my own. Of course, the servants were there to take care of my needs, but there was no one to keep me company. I would wander off in the mornings, taking some path up the hills, come back home for lunch, read a bit and then stroll off again till it was time for dinner. Sometimes I walked up to my grandparents' house, but it seemed so different now, with people I didn't know occupying the house.

The three-month winter break over, I was almost eager to return to my boarding school in Shimla.

It wasn't as though I had many friends at school. I needed a friend, but it was not easy to find one among a horde of rowdy, pea-shooting eighth formers, who carved their names on desks and stuck chewing gum on the class teacher's chair. Had I grown up with other children, I might have developed a taste for schoolboy anarchy; but in sharing my father's loneliness after his separation from my mother, and in being bereft of any close family ties, I had turned into a premature adult.

After a month in the eighth form, I began to notice a new boy, Omar, and then only because he was a quiet, almost taciturn person who took no part in the form's feverish attempt to imitate the Marx Brothers at the circus. He showed no resentment at the prevailing anarchy, nor did he make a move to participate in it. Once he caught me looking at him, and he smiled ruefully, tolerantly. Did I sense another adult in the class? Someone who was a little older than his years?

Even before we began talking to each other, Omar and I developed an understanding of sorts, and we'd nod almost respectfully to each other when we met in the classroom corridors or the environs of the dining hall or the dormitory. We were not in the same house. The house system practised its own form of apartheid, whereby a member of one house was expected not to fraternize with someone belonging to another. Those public schools certainly knew how to clamp you into compartments. However, these barriers vanished when Omar and I found ourselves selected for the School Colts' hockey team, Omar as a full-back, I as the goalkeeper.

The taciturn Omar now spoke to me occasionally, and we combined well on the field of play. A good understanding is needed between a goalkeeper and a full-back. We were on the same wavelength. I anticipated his moves, he was familiar with mine. Years later, when I read Conrad's *The Secret Sharer*, I thought of Omar.

It wasn't until we were away from the confines of school, classroom and dining hall that our friendship flourished. The hockey team travelled to Sanawar on the next mountain range, where we were to play a couple of matches against our old rivals, the Lawrence Royal Military School. This had been my father's old school, so I was keen to explore its grounds and peep into its classrooms.

Omar and I were thrown together a good deal during the visit to Sanawar, and in our more leisurely moments, strolling undisturbed around a school where we were guests and not pupils, we exchanged life histories and other confidences. Omar, too, had lost his father—had I sensed that before?—shot in some tribal encounter on the Frontier, for he hailed from the lawless lands beyond Peshawar. A wealthy uncle was seeing to Omar's education.

We wandered into the school chapel, and there I found my father's name—A.A. Bond—on the school's roll of honour board: old boys who had lost their lives while serving during the two World Wars.

'What did his initials stand for?' asked Omar.

'Aubrey Alexander.'

'Unusual names, like yours. Why did your parents call you Rusty?'

'I am not sure.' I told him about the book I was writing. It was my first one and was called *Nine Months* (the length of the school term, not a pregnancy), and it described some of the happenings at school and lampooned a few of our teachers. I had filled three slim exercise books with this premature literary project, and I allowed Omar to go through them. He must have been my first reader and critic.

'They're very interesting,' he said, 'but you'll get into trouble if someone finds them, especially Mr Fisher.'

I have to admit it wasn't great literature. I was better at hockey and football. I made some spectacular saves, and we won our matches against Lawrence Royal Military School. When we returned to Shimla, we were school heroes for a couple of days and lost some of our reticence; we were even a little more forthcoming with other boys. And then Mr Fisher, my housemaster, discovered my literary opus, *Nine Months*, under my mattress, and took it away and read it (as he told me later) from cover to cover. Corporal punishment then being in vogue, I was given six of the best with a springy Malacca cane, and my manuscript was torn up and deposited in Mr Fisher's wastepaper basket. All I had to show for my efforts were some purple welts on my bottom. These were proudly displayed to all who were interested, and I was a hero for another two days.

'Will you go away too when the British leave India?' Omar asked me one day.

'I don't think so,' I said. 'I don't have anyone to go back to in England, and my guardian, Mr Harrison, too seems to have no intention of going back.'

'Everyone is saying that our leaders and the British are going to divide the country. Shimla will be in India, Peshawar in Pakistan!'

'Oh, it won't happen,' I said glibly. 'How can they cut up such a big country?' But even as we chatted about the possibility, Nehru, Jinnah and Mountbatten, all those who mattered, were preparing their instruments for major surgery.

Before their decision impinged on our lives and everyone else's, we found a little freedom of our own, in an underground tunnel that we discovered below the third flat.

It was really part of an old, disused drainage system, and when Omar and I began exploring it, we had no idea just how far it extended. After crawling along on our bellies for some twenty feet, we found ourselves in complete darkness. Omar had brought along a small pencil torch, and with its help, we continued writhing forward (moving backwards would have been quite impossible) until we saw a glimmer of light at the end of the tunnel. Dusty, musty, very scruffy, we emerged at last on to a grassy knoll, a little way outside the school boundary.

It's always a great thrill to escape beyond the boundaries that adults have devised. Here we were in unknown territory. To travel without passports—that would be the ultimate in freedom!

But more passports were on their way—and more boundaries.

Lord Mountbatten, viceroy and governor-general-to-be, came for our Founder's Day and gave away the prizes. I had won a prize for something or the other and mounted the rostrum to receive my book from this towering, handsome man in his pinstripe suit. Bishop Cotton's was then the premier school of India, often referred to as the 'Eton of the East'. Viceroys and governors had graced its functions. Many of its boys had attained eminence in the civil services and armed forces. There was one 'old boy' about whom they maintained a stolid silence—General Dyer, who had ordered the massacre at Amritsar and destroyed the trust that had been building up between Britain and India.

Now Mountbatten spoke of the momentous events that were happening all around us—the War had just come to an end, the United Nations held out the promise of a world living in peace and harmony, and India, an equal partner with Britain, would be among the great nations...

A few weeks later, Bengal and the Punjab provinces were bisected. Riots flared up across northern India, and there was a great exodus of people crossing the newly drawn frontiers of Pakistan and India. Homes were destroyed, thousands lost their lives.

The common room radio and the occasional newspaper kept us abreast of events, but in our tunnel, Omar and I felt immune from all that was happening, worlds away from all the pillage, murder and revenge. And outside the tunnel, on the pine knoll below the school, there was fresh untrodden grass, sprinkled with clover and daisies; the only sounds we heard were the hammering of a woodpecker and the distant insistent call of the Himalayan Barbet. Who could touch us there?

'And when all the wars are done,' I said, 'a butterfly will still be beautiful.'

'Did you read that somewhere?'

'No, it just came into my head.'

'Already you're a writer.'

'No, I want to play hockey for India or football for Arsenal. Only winning teams!'

'You can't win forever. Better to be a writer.'

When the monsoon arrived, the tunnel was flooded, the drain choked with rubble. We were allowed out to the cinema to see Laurence Olivier's *Hamlet*, a film that did nothing to raise our spirits on a wet and gloomy afternoon; but it was our last picture that year because communal riots suddenly broke out in Shimla's Lower Bazaar, an area that was still much as Kipling had described it—'a man who knows his way there can defy all the police of India's summer capital'—and we were confined to school indefinitely.

One morning, after prayers in the chapel, the headmaster announced that the Muslim boys—those who had their homes in what was now Pakistan—would have to be evacuated, sent to their homes across the border with an armed convoy.

The tunnel no longer provided an escape for us. The bazaar was out of bounds. The flooded playing field was deserted. Omar and I sat on a damp wooden bench and talked about the future in vaguely hopeful terms, but we didn't solve any problems. Mountbatten, Nehru and Jinnah were doing all the solving.

It was soon time for Omar to leave—he left along with some fifty other boys from Lahore, Pindi and Peshawar. The rest of us—Hindus, Christians, Parsis—helped them load their luggage into the waiting trucks. A couple of boys broke down and wept. So did our departing school captain, a Pathan who had been known for his stoic and unemotional demeanour. Omar waved cheerfully to me and I waved back. We had vowed to meet again some day.

The convoy got through safely enough. There was only one casualty—the school cook, who had strayed into an off-limits area in the foothill town of Kalika and been set upon by a mob. He wasn't seen again.

Towards the end of the school year, just as we were all getting ready to leave for the school holidays, I received a letter from Omar. He told me something about his new school and how he missed my company and our games and our tunnel to freedom. I replied and gave him my home address, but I did not hear from him again.

Some seventeen or eighteen years later, I did get news of Omar, but in an entirely different context. India and Pakistan were at war, and in a bombing raid over Ambala, not far from Shimla, a Pakistani plane was shot down. Its crew died in the crash. One of them, I learnt later, was Omar.

Did he, I wonder, get a glimpse of the playing fields we knew so well as boys? Perhaps memories of his schooldays flooded back as he flew over the foothills. Perhaps he remembered the tunnel through which we were able to make our little escape to freedom.

But there are no tunnels in the sky.

THE WHISTLING SCHOOLBOY

The moon was almost full. Bright moonlight flooded the road. But I was stalked by the shadows of the trees, by the crooked oak branches reaching out towards me—some threateningly, others as though they needed companionship.

Once I dreamt that the trees could walk. That on moonlit nights like this they would uproot themselves for a while, visit each other, talk about old times—for they had seen many men and happenings, especially the older ones. And then, before dawn, they would return to the places where they had been condemned to grow. Lonely sentinels of the night. And this was a good night for them to walk. They appeared eager to do so: a restless rustling of leaves, the creaking of branches—these were sounds that came from within them in the silence of the night.

Occasionally other strollers passed me in the dark. It was still quite early, just eight o'clock, and some people were on their way home. Others were walking into town for a taste of the bright lights, shops and restaurants. On the unlit road, I could not recognize them. They did not notice me. I was reminded of an old song from my childhood. Softly, I began humming the tune, and soon the words came back to me:

We three,
We're not a crowd;
We're not even company—

My echo,
My shadow,
And me…

I looked down at my shadow, moving silently beside me. We take our shadows for granted, don't we? There they are, the uncomplaining companions of a lifetime, mute and helpless witnesses to our every act of commission or omission. On this bright, moonlit night I could not help noticing you, Shadow, and I was sorry that you had to see so much that I was ashamed of; but glad, too, that you were around when I had my small triumphs. And what of my echo? I thought of calling out to see if my call came back to me; but I refrained from doing so, as I did not wish to disturb the perfect stillness of the mountains or the conversations of the trees.

The road wound up the hill and levelled out at the top, where it became a ribbon of moonlight entwined between tall deodars. A flying squirrel glided across the road, leaving one tree for another. A nightjar called. The rest was silence.

The old cemetery loomed up before me. There were many old graves—some large and monumental—and there were a few recent graves too, for the cemetery was still in use. I could see flowers scattered on one of them—a few late dahlias and scarlet salvia. Further on near the boundary wall, part of the cemetery's retaining wall had collapsed in the heavy monsoon rains. Some of the tombstones had come down with the wall. One grave lay exposed. A rotting coffin and a few scattered bones were the only relics of someone who had lived and loved like you and me.

Part of the tombstone lay beside the road, but the lettering had worn away. I am not normally a morbid person, but something made me stoop and pick up a smooth round shard of bone, probably part of a skull. When my hand closed over it, the bone crumbled into fragments. I let them fall to the grass. Dust to dust. And from somewhere, not too far away, came the sound of someone whistling.

At first I thought it was another late-evening stroller whistling to himself, much as I had been humming my old song. But the whistler approached quite rapidly; the whistling was loud and cheerful. A boy on a bicycle sped past. I had only a glimpse of him, before his cycle went weaving through the shadows on the road.

But he was back again in a few minutes. And this time he stopped a few feet away from me, and gave me a quizzical half-smile. A slim dusky boy of fourteen or fifteen. He wore a school blazer and a yellow scarf. His eyes were pools of liquid moonlight.

'You don't have a bell on your cycle,' I said.

He said nothing, just smiled at me with his head a little to one side. I put out my hand, and I thought he was going to take it. But then, quite suddenly, he was off again, whistling cheerfully though rather tunelessly. A whistling schoolboy. A bit late for him to be out but he seemed an independent sort.

The whistling grew fainter, then faded away altogether. A deep sound-denying silence fell upon the forest. My shadow and I walked home.

Next morning I woke to a different kind of whistling—the song of the thrush outside my window. It was a wonderful day, the sunshine warm and sensuous, and I longed to be out in the open. But there was work to be done, proofs to be corrected, letters to be written. And it was several days before I could walk to the top of the hill, to that lonely tranquil resting place under the deodars. It seemed to me ironic that those who had the best view of the glistening snow-capped peaks were all buried several feet underground.

Some repair work was going on. The retaining wall of the cemetery was being shored up, but the overseer told me that there was no money to restore the damaged grave. With the help of the chowkidar, I returned the scattered bones to a little hollow under the collapsed masonry and left some money with him so that he could have the open grave bricked up. The name on the gravestone had worn away, but I could make out a date—20 November 1950—some fifty years ago, but not too long ago as gravestones go.

I found the burial register in the church vestry and turned back the yellowing pages to 1950, when I was just a schoolboy myself. I found the name there—Michael Dutta, aged fifteen—and the cause of death: road accident.

Well, I could only make guesses. And to turn conjecture into certainty, I would have to find an old resident who might remember the boy or the accident.

There was old Miss Marley at Pine Top. A retired teacher from Woodstock, she had a wonderful memory, and had lived in the hill station for more than half a century.

White-haired and smooth-cheeked, her bright blue eyes full of curiosity, she gazed benignly at me through her old-fashioned pince-nez.

'Michael was a charming boy—full of exuberance, always ready to oblige. I had only to mention that I needed a newspaper or an Aspirin, and he'd be off on his bicycle, swooping down these steep roads with great abandon. But these hills roads, with their sudden corners, weren't meant for racing around on a bicycle. They were widening our roads for motor traffic, and a truck was coming uphill, loaded with rubble, when Michael came round a bend and smashed headlong into it. He was rushed to the hospital, and the doctors did their best, but he did not recover consciousness. Of course, you must have seen his grave. That's why you're here. His parents? They left shortly afterwards. Went abroad, I think...A charming boy, Michael, but just a bit too reckless. You'd have liked him, I think.'

I did not see the phantom bicycle rider again for some time, although I felt his presence on more than one occasion. And when, on a cold winter's evening, I walked past that lonely cemetery, I thought I heard him whistling far away. But he did not manifest himself. Perhaps it was only the echo of a whistle, in communion with my insubstantial shadow.

It was several months before I saw that smiling face again. And then it came at me out of the mist as I was walking home in drenching monsoon rain. I had been to a dinner party at the old community centre, and I was returning home along a very narrow, precipitous path known as the Eyebrow. A storm had been threatening all evening. A heavy mist had settled on the hillside. It was so thick that the light from my torch simply bounced off it. The sky blossomed with sheet lightning and thunder rolled over the mountains. The rain became heavier. I moved forward slowly, carefully, hugging the hillside. There was a clap of thunder, and then I saw him emerge from the mist and stand in my way—the same slim dark youth who had materialized near the cemetery. He did not smile. Instead he put up his hand and waved at me. I hesitated, stood still. The mist lifted a little, and I saw that the path had disappeared. There was a gaping emptiness a few feet in front of me. And then a drop of over a hundred feet to the rocks below.

As I stepped back, clinging to a thorn bush for support, the boy vanished. I stumbled back to the community centre and spent the night on a chair in the library.

I did not see him again.

But weeks later, when I was down with a severe bout of flu, I heard him from my sickbed, whistling beneath my window. *Was he calling to me to join him*, I wondered, *or was he just trying to reassure me that all was well?* I got out of bed and looked out, but I saw no one. From time to time I heard his whistling; but as I got better, it grew fainter until it ceased altogether.

Fully recovered, I renewed my old walks to the top of the hill. But although I lingered near the cemetery until it grew dark, and paced up and down the deserted road, I did not see or hear the whistler again. I felt lonely, in need of a friend, even if it was only a phantom bicycle rider. But there were only the trees.

And so every evening I walk home in the darkness, singing the old refrain:

We three,
We're not alone,
We're not even company—
My echo,
My shadow,
And me…

MASTERJI

I was strolling along the platform, waiting for the arrival of the Amritsar Express, when I saw Mr Khushal, handcuffed to a policeman.

I hadn't recognized him at first—a paunchy gentleman with a lot of grey in his beard and a certain arrogant amusement in his manner. It was only when I came closer, and we were almost face to face, that I recognized my old Hindi teacher.

Startled, I stopped and stared. And he stared back at me, a glimmer of recognition in his eyes. It was over twenty years since I'd last seen him, standing jauntily before the classroom blackboard, and now here he was tethered to a policeman and looking as jaunty as ever…

'Good—good evening, sir,' I stammered, in my best public school manner. (You must always respect your teacher, no matter what the circumstances.)

Mr Khushal's face lit up with pleasure. 'So you remember me! It's nice to see you again, my boy.'

Forgetting that his right hand was shackled to the policeman's left, I made as if to shake hands. Mr Khushal thoughtfully took my right hand in his left and gave it a rough squeeze. A faint odour of cloves and cinnamon reached me, and I remembered how he had always been redolent of spices when standing beside my desk, watching me agonize over my Hindi–English translation.

He had joined the school in 1948, not long after the Partition. Until then there had been no Hindi teacher; we'd been taught Urdu and French. Then came a ruling that Hindi was to be a compulsory subject, and at the age of sixteen I found myself struggling with a new script. When Mr Khushal joined the staff (on the recommendation of a local official), there was no one else in the school who knew Hindi, or who could assess Mr Khushal's abilities as a teacher…

And now once again he stood before me, only this time he was in the custody of the law.

I was still recovering from the shock when the train drew in, and everyone on the platform began making a rush for the compartment doors. As the policeman elbowed his way through the crowd, I kept close behind him and his charge, and as a result I managed to get into the same third-class compartment. I found a seat right opposite Mr Khushal. He did not seem to be the least bit embarrassed by the handcuffs, or by the stares of his fellow passengers. Rather, it was the policeman who looked unhappy and ill at ease.

As the train got under way, I offered Mr Khushal one of the parathas made for me by my Ferozepur landlady. He accepted it with alacrity. I offered one to the constable as well, but although he looked at it with undisguised longing, he felt duty-bound to decline.

'Why have they arrested you, sir?' I asked. 'Is it very serious?'

'A trivial matter,' said Mr Khushal. 'Nothing to worry about. I shall be at liberty soon.'

'But what did you *do*?'

Mr Khushal leant forward. 'Nothing to be ashamed of,' he said in a confiding tone. 'Even a great teacher like Socrates fell foul of the law.'

'You mean—one of your pupils—made a complaint?'

'And why should one of my pupils make a complaint?' Mr

Khushal looked offended. 'They were the beneficiaries—it was for *them*.' He noticed that I looked mystified, and decided to come straight to the point: 'It was simply a question of false certificates.'

'Oh,' I said, feeling deflated. Public school boys are always prone to jump to the wrong conclusions…

'*Your* certificates, sir?'

'Of course not. Nothing wrong with my certificates—I had them printed in Lahore, in 1946.'

'With age comes respectability,' I remarked. 'In that case, whose…?'

'Why, the matriculation certificates I've been providing all these years to the poor idiots who would never have got through on their own!'

'You mean you gave them your own certificates?'

'That's right. And if it hadn't been for so many printing mistakes, no one would have been any wiser. You can't find a good press these days, that's the trouble… It was a public service, my boy, I hope you appreciate that… It isn't fair to hold a boy back in life simply because he can't get through some puny exam… Mind you, I don't give my certificates to *anyone*. They come to me only after they have failed two or three times.'

'And I suppose you charge something?'

'Only if they can pay. There's no fixed sum. Whatever they like to give me. I've never been greedy in these matters, and you know I am not unkind…'

Which is true enough, I thought, looking out of the carriage window at the green fields of Moga and remembering the half-yearly Hindi exam when I had stared blankly at the question paper, knowing that I was totally incapable of answering any of it. Mr Khushal had come walking down the line of desks and stopped at mine, breathing cloves all over me. 'Come on, boy, why haven't you started?'

'Can't do it, sir,' I'd said. 'It's too difficult.'

'Never mind,' he'd urged in a whisper. 'Do *something.* Copy it out, copy it out!'

And so, to pass the time, I'd copied out the entire paper, word for word. And a fortnight later, when the results were out, I found I had passed!

'But, sir,' I had stammered, approaching Mr Khushal when I found him alone. 'I never answered the paper. I couldn't translate the passage. All I did was copy it out!'

'That's why I gave you pass marks,' he'd answered imperturbably. 'You have such neat handwriting. If ever you do learn Hindi, my boy, you'll write a beautiful script!'

And remembering that moment, I was now filled with compassion for my old teacher; and leaning across, I placed my hand on his knee and said: 'Sir, if they convict you, I hope it won't be for long. And when you come out, if you happen to be in Delhi or Ferozepur, please look me up. You see, I'm still rather hopeless at Hindi, and perhaps you could give me tuition. I'd be glad to pay…'

Mr Khushal threw back his head and laughed, and the entire compartment shook with his laughter.

'Teach you Hindi!' he cried. 'My dear boy, what gave you the idea that I ever knew any Hindi?'

'But, sir—if not Hindi what were you teaching us all the time at school?'

'Punjabi!' he shouted, and everyone jumped in their seats. 'Pure Punjabi! But how were *you* to know the difference?'

www.ingramcontent.com/pod-product-compliance
Lightning Source LLC
Chambersburg PA
CBHW020025030726
47499CB00007B/2268
9789357021869